THE ROCK AND ROLL DIARIES

MAKING IT

JAMIE SCALLION

Book One of The Rock 'n' Roll Diaries series

THE ROCK 'N' ROLL DIARIES
A MADNOTES MEDIA PUBLICATION

First published in Great Britain and Ireland by Madnotes Media, 2013
This revised edition published 2015

Copyright © Jamie Scallion 2013

ISBN 978-0-9926855-1-5

A CIP catalogue record of this book is available from the British Library.

www.therocknrolldiaries.com

MAKING IT

Written: Jamie Scallion

Produced: Penny Luithlen

Mixed: Jill Sawyer Phypers

Artwork: Melinda Elek

A&R: Mark Sheehan and Danny O'Donoghue

General Manager: Rodney Alejandro

Label: Madnotes Media

Burt - 9th September

I, Burt Windsor, have everything. I have the looks, the style, the massive house, the cool friends, and of course all the girls.

If I had a CV, which I don't coz I'm fifteen, this would be the first sentence. I think it would definitely make people read about my shanizzle. I would defo get the job.

Except the last bit is a lie because I don't have the one thing I've wanted since I was eleven years old - Rebecca Vargas. First day I saw her I knew I had to make her mine. Back when I was a little Year 7 scrotum she was the fittest girl in class. Now she's the fittest girl in the school, and she's grown the best pair of tits.

I think long black hair, olive skin, green eyes and massive bangers is the perfect combination. There's only one thing on my bucket list and that's getting with Bex. So far it's been a disaster. #wellgutting.

The first time I tried was at the Year 7 Prom. She just said no. Then again in Year 8 at Zayn's New Year's Eve party she told me I was too cocky. In Year 9 it was on a school trip to Brighton. She said she didn't like spoilt little rich kids. Last year, older and totally wiser, I made my move up on High Bench in Greenwich Park, my favourite place in the world. It was proper romantic. I lured her there by saying I needed to talk to her about her mate Riana. Turned out Riana really fancied me, so all I did was stitch myself up. Every year, shot down like a a right proper idiot.

Now she has a long line of fools queuing up.
Some of them are my own mates. It can't happen.
It's Year 11 and this year I'm going for the
organic approach. I will become the boy she
wants. I will not give up. I must not fail.
The Burtmeister is ready.

SONG 1 ARRIVALS

"So is that it then?"

"What?"

"Final answer?"

"How many times do I have to say no, Burt?"

"I need some feedback this time. Is it my style you're not having? Coz it can't be my looks."

"Are you being serious?"

Bex looked him up and down. "OK, for starters I'm into rock bands. You dress like you're in a boy band. Look at those shoes!"

"What's wrong with them?"

"It's not about the shoes."

Bex rolled her eyes, turned and headed off to class. Burt watched her go. Had she no idea how good they would look together? *Boy band??* She had to be taking the mick. Did he really look like he was in a boy band? He needed time to think.

He headed for the school vegetable patch. The walled-off scrap of land was like a purpose-built sanctuary for skivers. Burt liked it there when everyone was in lessons. He sat down heavily on a moss-covered school chair.

Another advance totally shot down. Five years of striking out. An eternity. Something had to give. Persistence as a method was clearly failing. The whole school knew that he'd been after Bex for years. Even his mates were starting to give him major grief about it. As his gaze drifted across the dilapidated greenhouse, Burt considered his options.

The shoes could go. That was easy to sort. Suddenly it came to him; he would re-style his whole look. She liked rock. He would dress rock. How hard could it be? A leather jacket and some skinny jeans – maybe some cowboy boots. That might do the trick.

No. It wouldn't.

Burt concentrated hard. If he was going to get with Bex Vargas he needed to go way beyond the usual limits.

The idea hit him like a hurricane. He stood up, sending the chair crashing backwards into a withered tomato plant and ran inside.

Sitting alone in the lunch canteen was not something Edward Poacher, Egg to his fellow students, enjoyed, but his options were limited. He wasn't big, hard, cool or funny and he knew it. He accepted the geek label on day one of Year 7. His hair was an uncontrollable flame red; his skin pale and spotty. His mum chose the wire-framed glasses and cheap clothes. At over six feet tall it was impossible to remain anonymous despite the deliberate stoop. This unfortunate combination attracted the attention of nearly every bully in the year, whilst the female half of the school had no idea he even existed.

Music was Egg's life. He could play any instrument he picked up. By the age of ten he was grade eight on the piano. Every spare moment was taken up with new discovery; no stone was left unturned in the unearthing of musical master-pieces. Classical, rock, roots, alternative – if it was good then Egg would find it. Music and the monotony of the school routine were his friends.

As he sat there sucking the life out of a carton of value orange juice, Egg watched the cool kids as they laughed and joked. He watched Rebecca Vargas. Perfect in every way, and so far out of his league he felt guilty just looking at her. Her smile alone sent a tingling sensation up his neck and into his head. What would happen if she smiled directly at him? He didn't know, but he thought he might like to find out.

Burt stared at Egg and began to have serious doubts. Could he really be in a band with this kid? He scanned the hall, hoping no one would spot him on the wrong side of the canteen. Bex was with Riana, looking disgracefully fit. Adapt and compromise. He needed to get to work.

Burt quick-stepped his way over. "Hello, mate!" he said brightly.

Egg looked up from his salad sandwich in surprise. It was the first time he had seen the best-looking boy in the school up close. He scanned the features for flaws; the cheekbones, strong jaw and dazzling blue eyes. There were none. What could Burt Windsor possibly want with him?

"You any good?" Burt asked casually, pointing to the tuba case under the dining table.

"I'm grade eight," Egg replied, blushing.

"You know how to play guitar, right?"

"Yes. Why?"

"I heard you were pretty useful."

"I'm OK."

Burt took a deep breath and cleared his throat. "I'm starting a band and I'm looking for a lead guitarist, so I thought I might as well ask you," he said.

Egg shifted in his seat. "You up for it then?" Burt pressed.

Egg was silent for a long moment before cautiously nodding.

"Cool! We're holding auditions for a bass player and drummer next Tuesday in the assembly room after school. Me and you will be the judging panel. Good cop, bad cop. Like on the *Starfinder* panel… It's a show on TV."

Burt balled his hand and thrust it toward Egg. "Deal?"

Egg stared at the fist for a moment. Confused, he extended an open palm. Burt sighed and shook his head. He nudged the back of Egg's fingers and sauntered back to his friends.

Egg continued to watch the cool kids, but something had changed. Colour started to seep into his black-and-white life. His mind buzzed, excited by new possibilities.

Burt – 12th September

I have to get with Bex soon or I'll go mental.
I have an iPhone picture of her in her P.E. kit
that helps. I bought a bunch of new clothes and
asked her on a date, but she just laughed and
walked off again. I ran after her and asked if
she was winding me up? She told me I couldn't
just put on a leather jacket and think I was
rock'n'roll, I had to live it. So I told her I
was in a band. She told me I was only a 6/10 in
the looks department, but if I really was in a
band then I might be a 10/10. 6/10? That's gotta
be a wind up! Telling me I look like I'm in a
boy band is one thing, but saying I'm six out
of ten is a proper cuss. The challenge remains,
scoring a perfect ten on the Bex Fit-O-Meter is
fundamental. Anyway – she has no idea how well
hot my band is gonna be.

I asked this pleb called Egg to help me. He's
a right ginger geek but I had no choice. I need
someone who can play an instrument. It's got
proper drastic now. I'm on full alert.

It's all kicking off next week. I'm holding
auditions and Egg is going to judge them with
me. My old man tells me every chance he gets
I'm "style over substance" and that I've never
done anything of value in my life. I'm fifteen.
What does he expect? Being "cool as" is the only
thing anyone cares about. I tried to explain
that to him but he just looked at me as if I
wasn't there. That he didn't get my point makes
him the knobhead. I've got substance and I'm
going to do something of value. So bollocks to
you, Dad. How about you and Mum start giving
me parental advice when you're actually in the
country longer than five minutes.

The back of the upper deck was the most dangerous place on earth, exactly why Michael Twining, AKA Tea, made a point of being there. He sat on the hard plastic seat and sparked a joint. He inhaled deeply, tipped his head back, exhaled and wondered why he hadn't tagged anything in over a year. As the blue smoke hit the ceiling of the empty bus, Tea pulled out his iPod and spun the dial. Public Enemy. He turned the classic full up.

Had he grown out of tagging? Was he evolving? His mum wouldn't complain if he was. Tea loved his mum. She let him smoke in the flat, have girls back and since his dad had abandoned him he was allowed out as late as he liked. Tea didn't take advantage of the freedom.

Sometimes he caught her staring out of the window at the worn-out estate below with a sad look on her face. He didn't like seeing her like that. He was mad at his dad for leaving them so badly in debt. Uncle Frank, his mum's brother, tried to help as much as possible but mostly it was Tea and his mum against the world.

Tea tensed when he saw Burt Windsor lurch up the aisle toward him. What did he want? The back of the bus was no place for a pretty boy. Was he going to tell Tea to put the joint out? He hadn't figured Burt as a do-gooder. A massive poser, yes, but not a do-gooder.

Burt said nothing, and coolly handed him a flier. It read:

Members needed for well amazing new rock band. Auditions to be held on Tuesday 18th September after school in the Music Room – only serious applicants need apply.

Tea sat up from his slumped position. If there was one thing he took seriously, one thing he did better than smoking weed, it was playing bass guitar. His Fender Precision was the only thing his father had ever given him. It was the only legal thing his father had ever taught him.

Egg trudged up the steepest hill in South London towards school. The September morning had a chill in the air. It was bad enough that his coat was too thin, without his tuba weighing him down, slapping the back of his legs. He heard a shout from behind.

"Oi! Smeg!"

The tuba made it difficult to look round. Egg knew it was George Graves, his chief tormentor. George got away with pushing people around because he was in Burt Windsor's gang, the LBC. He was good looking, popular and the meanest bully in Year 11.

"All right, Pasty Face? You been chatting with dead people again?" George sneered, skipping up alongside Egg and giving him a hard clap on the back of his neck. Egg barrelled forward, just managing to keep his balance.

"You gonna audition for the band?" George asked, his breath visible in harsh wisps.

"I'm not auditioning for anything. I don't know what you're talking about," Egg lied, shooting George a quick glance.

George hadn't bothered John Lewis for his school uniform. Black shoes, white shirt, house tie and blue trousers were replaced by black moccasins without socks, slim-fit dark blue jeans, a white Fred Perry polo shirt and a custom-made burgundy house tie. He had flawless skin, a year-round tan and shoulder-length blonde hair. George had been voted the second best-looking boy in the year. Egg suspected he dyed his hair so he could look more like Burt. Some reckoned he plucked his dark eyebrows too. Either way, Egg thought George's dead blue eyes were set too deep, giving him a hollow, almost starved look.

"Burt tells me you're pretty good on guitar."

"Does he?"

"Yeah. Mind you he also said you're the biggest tit in London Town so don't get too excited."

Egg quickened his pace. George stepped behind and kicked at Egg's heels. He crashed face first, his tuba hammering the back of his head as he clattered to the pavement. George bounced away, laughing.

Clipper bombed up the wing, skinned the right back, cut inside and flew a perfectly weighted ball onto his centre forward's head. Burt's finishing was beautiful; goal number four. Clipper ran over and grabbed his team-mate for the fourth time that day, squeezing him hard around the waist.

Back in the changing room Clipper studied Burt's midriff. It was mental how ripped he was. He glanced at the other boys as they changed. None of them were anywhere near as defined. Burt looked up and Clipper dropped his eyes.

"You played good today, Clip," Burt shouted over the chat. "When are your trials for Charlton Youth again?"

"Next Thursday!" Clipper answered, unable to meet his teammate's eye.

"You play drums, don't you?" Burt asked, strutting over to Clipper and handing him a flier.

Clipper read it slowly. He and Burt didn't chat off the pitch. Burt had the LBC. Clipper hung with the football heads. "Er … yes," he replied before bolting out of the changing room.

The corner shop on the estate where Justin Liam Clipper lived was his safe spot; the place he visited when he needed to work stuff out. Clipper loved to surf the chocolate counter before checking out the magazine racks. Why was he so shy around Burt? He couldn't be in a band with the kid unless he got a grip on it.

The ritual was always the same: pick up football magazine, flick, put down; quick look around, pick up fashion magazine, study heavily. Clipper could easily spend an hour in the corner shop. The shop owner didn't mind because he was such a likeable lad.

Clipper wondered what he would look like in some of the clothes he saw in the magazines. His eye was drawn to some of the more eccentric looks. Why didn't he just buy one? No one would care, would they? And even if they did, he was the hardest lad in the school; unbeaten in seven fights.

His most recent scrap had been with a lad called George Graves, and was the fight that confirmed Clipper's status. George was an evil git who picked on kids smaller or weaker than him. Clipper hated bullies. His dad had been bullied for years at school.

It made no odds to Clipper that George was a member of the LBC. No one was untouchable if they were throwing their weight around. It started when George spammed a geeky lad who was on his own in the dining hall. Clipper offered him out and George accepted the challenge. The venue and time was set, the underpass after the last bell. The centre of the subway was open air, with four tunnelled exits surrounding steep grassy slopes. It was the closest thing to a gladiatorial amphitheatre the kids had.

Everyone bunched up tight on the grassy banks. No one wanted to miss the fight of the year. George was beaten in forty seconds and the crowd loved every moment. Clipper was the new Daddy of the School.

No one would ever bother Clipper, so why was he worried that people might discover his secret passion for fashion?

The morning after the big game Clipper arrived at school tired and stiff. The flier Burt had shown him in the changing rooms had kept him awake. He checked the game report on the bulletin board and noticed that beneath it, stuck up with chewing gum, was the same flier. He read it again, took a deep breath and made a decision.

SONG 2 AUDITIONS

Egg stood on the sweeping gravel drive and studied the enormous house. How could people live in such luxury? What did they do with all that space? Egg would only need a music room and a bedroom. Maybe a kitchen and a bathroom too. This house had three floors and sixteen outward-facing windows.

Three vehicles were parked on the driveway. Egg didn't know much about cars, but he recognised the brands of Lamborghini and Porsche. He'd seen the large silver Range Rover before, because last term Burt had driven it to school and parked it next to the headmaster's Kia. Burt had been suspended for a week.

Egg found it hard to go up the grandiose steps leading to the front door; not physically but mentally. Ever since Burt had asked him to be in a band Egg had worried. He worried about what his mum would say. He worried about not being good enough, and he worried about being accepted by Burt's friends. He'd slept really badly since Burt had insisted he come to the house for a band meeting. He'd spent an hour picking over his wardrobe, trying to decide what he should wear.

Suddenly the door swung open. Egg spun quickly and started back down the steps.

"Egg, what are you doing?"

He froze and turned slowly back towards the voice, his face scarlet. "Oh, I … I forgot something."

"What?" Burt said leaning casually on the door-frame.

"Er… My guitar."

"I told you yesterday I have loads of guitars. I have everything."

"Yes, I can see that." Egg relaxed a little and nodded at the mansion. "It's very nice."

"It's yours for 3.3 million." Burt said, smiling. "Come in. Let's get on with it."

Inside the house Egg felt as though his neck was made of rubber. Taking in the wealth was exhausting; the china vases, the decorative mirrors, the plush rugs and the ornate pieces of antique furniture. The stairway that dominated the entrance and rose up to the first floor was at least five times wider than his stairs at home. He shook his head and followed Burt along a marble corridor to a kitchen. Except it didn't look like any kitchen Egg had ever seen. It was huge. A massive square island work-surface stood in the centre of the room, with lots of shiny pots, pans and kitchen utensils hanging over it on metal hooks. On the other side of the room in the bay of the enormous double windows was the dining area with a beautifully carved round table at its heart. Sitting at the table was a tiny figure; a girl of about nine or ten, with loads of wavy hair and blue plastic-framed glasses. Her presence was completely unexpected.

"Hi," said the girl.

"Hello, I'm Edward but everyone calls me Egg," he replied, rooted to the spot.

She smiled, her eyes fixed on him with intense curiosity. "You don't look like Burt's usual friends. Do you want a drink?"

"Oh OK. Water, please."

"Don't fuss over him, Mills. We're here to talk important business."

"Music business?" she said, skipping to the double-door fridge. "How could you possibly know that?"

"I read stuff on your laptop," she said, filling an elegant glass from a magic dispenser.

Burt shook his head. "How many times do I have to tell you? That's private. Can you not read it, please?"

Millie handed Egg the water. "Are you the best musician in the school?"

"I wouldn't say that!"

"What instruments can you play?"

"Well. Let me see." Egg smiled for the first time. "I play the piano, guitar, violin and tuba to a pretty high standard. I also took tabla lessons for a while, which is an Indian percussive instrument. I think I could probably play most instruments to be honest. You see if you master a wind, percussive, stringed, plucked, plonked and bowed instrument you pretty much have all bases covered."

Millie let out a burst of laughter. It was infectious and Egg snorted some of his water back up. Immediately mortified, he stared at the floor.

"All right, Egg, she didn't ask for your life story. Do you wanna come and check out the music room?" Burt said impatiently.

"Good to meet you, Edward the Egg," Millie said.

Egg drained the water and hurried over to the sink. He wanted to wash the glass, but one glance at the space age tap with its single lever put him off the idea. There was no draining board, just a hole in the granite surface. He placed the glass carefully down on the side.

"Jesus, Smeg, you really are well trained," Burt said, disappearing back towards the giant hall. Egg followed him up the stairs, taking in the immaculate landings with yet more beautiful furniture and ornaments.

"Where are your mum and dad?" Egg asked as they headed up towards the top of the house.

"Not here," Burt replied flatly. "They vanish for months on end."

"So who looks after you and Millie?"

"No one. I convinced my dad I was two years older than I am and that he could save money getting rid of the live-in housekeepers. We got the whole house to ourselves. The cleaner comes in three times a week and we get a weekly food delivery. That's it."

Egg frowned. "But he must know how old you are. What about your mum?"

Burt carried on up the stairs as he replied. "He probably does but what you gotta understand is my dad doesn't give a toss. And neither does she. Me and Mills don't need them anyway. We're fine."

Egg sensed this was a subject Burt wasn't keen on talking about. He swallowed his curiosity and followed Burt up the final flight of stairs.

The music room was on the third floor. He stood in the doorway and marvelled. Burt had every type of instrument imaginable.

"Is that a bouzouki?" Egg said, stepping into the room in wonder.

"Egg, I have no idea what you're talking about."

Egg paced across the cluttered room and extracted the stringed instrument from its wall mounting. He hitched up his leg, settled his foot on the piano stool and began to finger pick. A sharp metallic sound emanated from the instrument. Burt's eyes widened.

"It's Greek! From the lute family!" Egg said, unable to stop playing.

"I don't care where it's from, Egg, but you really can play the thing."

Burt - 18th September

I have an immaculate reputation. The looks, the clobber, the gang of loyal followers and a fleet of badass cars to drive (found the new hiding place for the keys, Dad! You really are a dick). I've been voted "fittest male" every year since I started secondary school. So why doesn't Bex want to get with me? It's not even logical.

The auditions are today! Mum's been away for two months and gets back tomorrow for two days. She hasn't even bothered to ask me what I want for my sixteenth birthday that's been and gone. Would have been good to see her longer than two days, but who needs parents when you're in a rock'n'roll band?! Egg came round yesterday. He's a total weirdo but he can properly play and he was well impressed with my music room. I reckon

my dad collecting all them instruments is about
the only useful thing he has ever done for me.
Even though it wasn't on purpose.

Egg hadn't moved from his chair for two hours. He hadn't been allowed to. He needed a pee so badly he'd started getting pains shooting from his bladder to his stomach.

Burt checked his clipboard. "OK, three more to see."

Burt had arranged with Mr Andrews to use the music room for the auditions and was taking it all very seriously. He'd put himself and Egg behind a table. Egg had choked back any honest comment throughout the unfolding pantomime. He finally snapped. Whether it was the pain erupting in his gut or the offence to his ears he wasn't sure.

"Burt, I just think this is madness. We've been sitting here for hours auditioning people that can't play and can't sing! It's pointless."

Burt looked incensed. "You what?!" Burt spat. "Just because you're all amazing at instruments don't mean every other tithead is. Get back in your box and do what I'm paying you to do."

"You're not paying me and yesterday at your home you said you wanted me to speak my mind and use my expertise to advise you."

Burt frowned. "So, what if I did?!"

"So, the only people we've been auditioning have been your talentless friends."

Burt looked outraged. "You're totally crossing the line now!" He slapped the table hard, making Egg jump. "They might be

18

talentless but at least they have a dress sense." Burt took a deep breath. "What about Sid Vicious or Stuart Sutcliff? They couldn't play but they looked great!"

Egg raised a hand in surrender. "OK, you said three more. Who's next?"

"George Graves!"

Egg put his head in his hands, his stomach lurching with renewed pain. George sauntered in arrogantly and gave Egg a wink.

"What's your name and where do you come from?" Burt asked him as soon as George was stood on the designated spot.

"You know my name, Burt, and you also know where I live," he replied with a mocking grin.

"Yes, yes, but for the benefit of my fellow judge please can you state your name and where you come from."

"I'm not stating my name and where I come from for his benefit."

Burt turned to Egg. "Do you know George?"

"He helps me carry my tuba up the hill from time to time," Egg said quietly.

"Oh!" Burt said looking very confused before turning back to George. "What will you be playing for us today?"

"Can't play anything. Gonna sing!"

"What are you going to sing?"

"'Who Shot the Sheriff' by Bob Marley."

Before Burt could reply George launched into an acapella interpretation of the song; a tuneless, disjointed dirge that was agony on the ears. Just as George was starting on the second verse Burt put a hand up.

"That's great, George. We'll let you know."

Egg watched, with some pleasure, as George's expression switched from concentration to confusion to humiliation in a couple of seconds. He glared at Egg and stomped out of the room.

"That went well!" Egg said.

Burt ignored him. "Next up is Clipper. He's the captain of the footie team and Daddy of the School."

"What's a Daddy of the School?" Egg asked.

Burt looked annoyed. "The hardest kid in school. Anyway, he is supposed to be a decent drummer. That's why I got you to set the drums up."

A barrel-chested boy with sandy hair, big eyebrows and a friendly face walked in. He wore training gear and was carrying a pair of drumsticks. It was obvious to Egg that he was extremely nervous.

"Hi, can you state your name and where you come from?" Burt said.

"I'm Clipper and I'm from here," he said, staring at his big white trainers.

Burt let out a long sigh and scraped a hand over his face. "OK, can you go and sit at the drums please, Clip, and show us what you got."

Clipper sat behind the kit. He closed his eyes, lifted a knuckle-white ham fist and began to play a three over four polyrhythm beat. At the same time he used his right foot to pedal the bass drum and his left for the high-hat.

Egg looked at Burt with raised eyebrows. "He's actually not bad."

Burt nodded in response, watching his team-mate intently. When he'd finished, Clipper shot up from his stool and almost sprinted back to the judging spot, red-faced.

"OK, Clip, we'll let you know. Thank you for coming."

Clipper gritted his teeth and shut his eyes tight. "Aren't you going to comment?" He paused. "No, don't comment, I know I was rubbish. I shouldn't have come."

Egg glanced from Burt to Clipper. "You're the best person we've seen all day," he said.

Clipper looked up, a smile spreading across his face. "Really? You mean it?"

"Yes, we do, now get out!" Burt said, glaring at Egg.

Clipper approached the table and shook both judges' hands. "Thanks loads for this opportunity," he said before turning and half jogging, half skipping out of the room.

"Who's next?" Egg asked innocently.

"Don't ever do that again. We absolutely can't give these people false hope."

Egg forced the laughter down. "Yes, you're right. Who's next?"

"Tea. He's a year older than us but Mr Andrews says he's an amazing bass player. He's from the estate. His Uncle is Frankie 'The Hat' Sheehan."

"I don't know who that is. Is he a celebrity?"

"No, he's not a celebrity," Burt sighed, shaking his head. "Anyway Tea rates himself pretty highly. The birds think he's proper good-looking, but he keeps to himself. I can't work him out. He's turned up to a couple of my parties with some random fitty on his arm. I think he must…" Before Burt could continue Tea strolled in wearing baggy jeans and big trainers. He was handsome but moody looking; the opposite of Clipper, with olive skin and long, glossy, straight black hair.

He put down the case he was carrying, unclipped it and removed an ancient but pristine guitar. He took the jack lead and plugged it in, slung the strap around his neck and began to play. Tea's fingers hurtled across the four fat strings, the deep rich sound he produced faultless. Egg watched, becoming increasingly excited. Burt put his palm up. Tea glanced at the hand, turned away and began to play high bass, the upper frets giving him the license to express more defined melody. After a minute he finished off with a flamboyant trill, turned back to the judging table and gave Burt an even stare. Burt put his hand down.

"Er, thank you very much. We'll let you know," he said.

Tea nodded, unslung his strap and started to reverse the process.

"Is that a 1966 Fender blacktop?" Egg almost whispered the question.

Tea looked up from his crouched position, closed the case on the instrument and nodded.

"Wow, that's some guitar," Egg gushed.

"It was the only thing my loser of an old man left me," Tea said, his voice deep and husky. "That and how to play the thing."

"Well, you certainly can play it," Egg said, blushing.

Tea nodded, glanced at Burt with unveiled scorn and left the room.

Egg turned to Burt excitedly. "He's the best player we've seen. I don't think he has any idea just how good he is!"

Burt wrinkled his perfect features. "I'm not sure he's the right fit!"

"Why not? He's the only one who can play. He's exactly the right fit."

Burt made for the door. "I need a slash."

Egg – 19th September
The auditions were yesterday. The standard was low and Burt was very annoying. He likened himself to Wilson Cloom from that TV show *Next Big Thing* but when it came to commenting on them he was very positive, probably because all except two were in the LBC. I really must find out what that stands for. Spencer, Christian, Zayn and of course George all auditioned. They were all rubbish.

When Tea walked in it was like a breath of fresh air. He was really cool. He didn't say a word, just started laying down great bass lines. I felt a pang of hope. My only critique would be that he puts slightly too many notes into each bar but he could obviously really play.

Just before Tea we had Clipper. He was really nervous. As soon as he started bashing I was reminded of a John Lennon quote. When he was asked if Ringo Star was the best drummer in the world, he replied "He's not even the best drummer in the Beatles".

I'm a better drummer than Clipper, but I can't play all the instruments in the band. Besides I'm pretty sure he will learn fast and has enough natural rhythm. I told Burt I think he should also be asked to join. Last year Clipper stuck up for me when George spammed me in the canteen. I don't think he even knew I was the same kid. I didn't see the fight, but I heard Clipper smashed him.

Before eventually agreeing on Clipper and Tea, Burt spent ages trying to convince me that some of his mates were good enough to play in the band. I wasn't having any of it. Brian Clough, the legendary football manager, once said. "We talk about it for twenty minutes and then we decide I was right." I don't like football but I do like good quotes.

Burt asked me to choose some songs for us to get stuck into at our first rehearsal. I tried to choose some that are both easy and are classics. I deliberately steered clear of modern songs:

Led Zeppelin – Black Dog; Guns 'n' Roses – Knocking On Heaven's Door; The Who – My Generation; The Beatles – Get Back; Steppenwolf – Born To Be Wild; Free – All Right Now; Jimi Hendrix – Voodoo Chile; Thin Lizzy – The Boys Are Back In Town

Last night I dreamt of Burt's music room. It was a very strange dream. Burt had a head the size of a cathedral and was standing up on the grand piano. Me, Clipper and Tea were all sitting cross-legged on the floor looking up at him as he sang Rod Stewart's Do You Think I'm Sexy. I awoke

with one question on my mind. What exactly would
Burt do in the band? Is it his intention to sing?

Tea – 20th September
The idiot known as Burt from the year below
asked, via Twitter, if I wanted to join his
poxy band today so I asked him a few relevant
questions.

1. How many gigs have you got booked?
2. Where would we practise?
3. How much do I get a week?
4. Did he expect me to dress in those stupid
jeans?
5. What's the band's name?

I forgot all the other answers because the band
name was so lame. The RockAteers? Who comes up
with a name like that? A massive weapon is who!
What a whack name and why is there a random
capital A in the middle of the name? He begged
me to join so I said yes. Why waste the talent?
Burt is just about the most confident bloke I have
ever seen, and the girls he hangs about with
are proper fit. I've decided I will skin it and
bling it until I can't be bothered no more and
then I can just piss off and leave them to it.
Clipper the drummer and Egg the guitarist are odd
choices. Basically the band consists of a plank,
an arrogant ponce and a fat footballer.

I have finally mastered how to roll a spliff with
one hand!

25

Clipper – 21st September

I got the gig! Get in! I'm the new drummer in
an awesome new rock band! How totally amazing
is that? First rehearsal is next week, I cannot
wait. Factoid!

GOD I LOVE THE NAME! We already sound like Rock
Stars.

Burt – 22nd September

I'm more than a bit chuffed with myself. In
only two weeks I have formed a rock band single-
handed! #getin! The line-up will be me in the
lead singer position. Egg on guitar, Tea on bass
and Clipper on drums. Not exactly the quartet I
imagined, but then if all my mates are gonna turn
out to be talentless tools what can I do?

What was Spencer doing singing a pre-puberty
Justin Bieber song? I had high hopes George
would be half-decent but he was even more
dreadful than everyone combined. He absolutely
murdered a Bob Marley song and in my book that's
sacrilege. Egg, the little ginger geek, didn't
do what I told him to do in the audition, but I
suppose he was right about Tea and Clipper. They
can both play. So that's it. I'm in a rock band.
Bex won't know what's hit her.

SONG 3 REHEARSALS

"If being in this band starts to impact on your school work it's over," were the words Egg heard as he left the house to go to rehearsal.

He took the shortcut through Greenwich Park, his mother's ultimatum ringing in his ears as he walked, his nerves building as he got closer to school. He pushed the anxiety down and considered the assembled group. The footballer, the bad boy, the poser and the geek; it was an interesting cocktail. Egg wasn't keen on being referred to as a geek but he'd given up trying to evade it. The worry started to build again. He didn't fit in.

He stopped outside the school dining-hall and took a series of deep gulping breaths. He put his guitar case down and held up his hands. They were shaking visibly. "You can do this, Egg," he reassured himself, before taking one final breath and pushing through the heavy double doors.

The dining-hall looked totally different cleared of all the chairs, tables and kids. Egg stood just inside the door and watched the activity in the centre of the room. Drums were being set up, guitar amps wheeled about, leads plugged in.

"You're late!" Burt shouted, looking up from the mass of wires that resembled a plate of black spaghetti.

"You are late, Egg, but you are also bang on time!" Tea said with a grin, nodding toward Burt's tangled equipment.

"Why don't we let Egg set up his own gear first?" Clipper said, frowning.

Egg hung his head and made his way over to the pristine guitar amp Burt had lent him. He started unravelling wire, flicking switches and plugging in leads. Within minutes he was ready to play. He stood patiently, ready to play, watching his band mates scratch their heads and pace around their gear – all borrowed from Burt's Aladdin's cave of a music room.

"Oi, Smeg, don't just stand there with your thumb up your crack. Go and help Clipper," Burt shouted.

Clipper stood over his incomplete drum kit, looking perplexed as he tried to feed a butterfly nut onto the cymbal stand. "Sorry, mate. I have 'em set up permanently at home. I can't remember how me and Dad sorted them out."

"It's fine, I'll have a go." Egg took the cymbals off the stands, collapsed the high-hat and reset everything.

"How come you know how to do all this?" Clipper asked.

Egg shrugged. "My old man was in a band. He and my mum made me learn piano and classical guitar from the age of five," he said, placing the final cymbal on its stand and smiling at Clipper. "He keeps loads of his old gear in the garage: drums, amps and all sorts. Learning drums and electric guitar is a lot more interesting than piano."

"What was your old man's band called?"

"I can't tell you."

"Why not?"

"Because it's a really stupid name."

"Can't be any worse than The RockAteers," Tea shouted from across the room.

Egg turned to Clipper. "Who are The RockAteers?"

"We are," Clipper replied giving Egg a friendly nudge in the arm. "Isn't it awesome?"

"What's wrong with The RockAteers?" Burt shouted, defensively. "Like to see you come up with a better name!"

"Why does it have a pointless capital 'A' in the middle of it?" Tea asked. "It's a rocket taking off!" Burt replied.

Tea rolled his eyes.

"Ok, so, let me rephrase. Why does it have a pointless rocket taking off in the middle of it!?"

Burt waved Tea away and returned to his equipment. The singer still hadn't managed to get a squeak out of his amp and was getting increasingly frustrated.

"What a piece of crap," he said, giving the amp a sharp kick.

Egg started towards him.

"Get lost, Egg, I don't need your help," Burt said with a dismissive wave of his hand.

Egg returned to his amp, slung the guitar around his neck and pumped his floor tuner. He started with some light finger trills, his digits moving fast over the six strings. The sound arguing tunelessly with Tea's bass.

"Piss off Egg, don't start showing off," Tea barked, his arms by his sides as he stared in aggressive wonder at Egg's graceful left hand.

The young guitarist stopped, his face reddening.

"Don't stop, Egg, keep playing, it's amazing." Clipper said, grinning.

"OK," he replied. "But you guys join in? Tea, why don't you give me something solid in A?" Egg paused. "In four four?"

The bassist scowled. "OK, but you might have a job keeping up."

Tea rattled out a firm, if busy, low line. Clipper clashed his sticks four times and joined him with a simple bass-drum heart beat.

Egg shut his eyes and started wailing, the thud of the drum and thump of the bass transporting him out of the school and away. Minutes passed before he opened his eyes again.

There smiling at him, in the doorway, was Rebecca Vargas, her face full of delight and expectation. She marched over to him and stuck out a hand.

"I'm Bex, how you doin'? You're totally wicked on that thing!"

Egg opened his mouth to speak, before hanging his head.

"You don't mind if I stick around do you, boys?" Bex said, unperturbed.

Burt shrugged in response and stood glaring at Egg, his arms folded, his guitar and amp still lifeless on the school-hall floor.

"Well, don't just stand there; give me a hand with this equipment," he told Egg.

Eventually they started up again. Egg, with his back to Bex, closed his eyes once more. Suddenly something caused him to open them again. Something far worse than the sound they were already making. Burt had started to sing.

Egg – 26th September
Just got back from our first ever rehearsal! It
sounded God-awful! I didn't know what to do.
Should I keep time with the hundred notes a
minute bass, or the out-of-time drummer?

Until it actually happened I really had no idea
what Burt would do in the band. When he started
singing I honestly thought he was joking. Not
only was he out of tune by a very huge margin,
but he seemed to be making up the words.
"Knocking On Heaven's Door": "Rama take these
bums from me, we can't feed them any more" is
what I heard. He kept on shouting the wrong words
at the top of his voice throughout the practice
and suddenly it became clear to me. I have joined
the worst band in history.

It's not just Burt – our rhythm section needs
work. They were OK when we were jamming, but once
we started learning the cover songs the cracks
started to show – more like giant craters.

The problem was that they only listened to their
own instrument so we were totally out of time
with each other, and we were also completely out
of tune. I tried to explain all this but was
pretty much ignored.

To make matters worse all of a sudden Bex Vargas
walked in. My God, she really is beautiful. She
has these amazing sparkling green eyes and cat-
like makeup. She is slim but she has big boobs.
I don't want to disrespect her like the others
would. I think she's the perfect size actually.
She has olive skin and jet black hair which she
wears up in a ponytail a lot of the time, but

last night she let it down. It was all full and shiny and a little bit wavy. The room totally transformed with her in it. I not only lost the power of speech but actually turned my back on her. How horrific! I just stood there with my back to the loveliest girl in the school whilst we made our dreadful racket and I stayed like that until she left. No one said a word about it. I can only assume that my reputation is so odd that this type of behaviour is expected.

At nine o'clock Burt said it was time for us to get out. As we packed up our equipment we had to endure the mad ravings of an obvious delusional.

"I thought we were blinding today, lads. We'll be earning millions in no time."

Burt may be a deluded fool but I was the idiot that chose to join the worst band in living memory.

Burt - 26th September
The first rehearsal with the band was awesome. What a day! Bex turned up and she looked mega hot! It's a matter of days before I tap that! Why would she turn up if she doesn't fancy me? Egg is one moody idiot, but he is well good on guitar. We were massive. I'm thinking about just being the singer. It's really hard playing guitar and singing all at the same time.

I can't wait till next week's rehearsal! Tea's a pleb. He can't stop playing loads of notes.

We had a row about me saying the bass is not a
melodic instrument. He reckons it is. Clipper
took his side. Anyway I don't care. I'm in a cool
arse rock'n'roll band and Bex is loving it large.

My mum is back for two days. I told her all about
it but she didn't give a monkey's. Mills did
though. (Mills, if you're reading this please can
you not? It's not appropriate for a girl your age!)

✪

As the weeks passed Egg grew increasingly frustrated with his band mates' lack of musical skill. How could their enthusiasm grow with every practice? It was baffling. True, they had showed some progress, but he knew their unwillingness to listen was holding them back. It wasn't how he had imagined his first band. Egg had dreamt of being in a group where each member was a genius. He wanted to be Radiohead, not a terrible pub covers band. He consoled himself that The RockAteers were a means to an end and he decided to stick with it.

As time passed Egg marked progress. Sometimes it was musical fluke, other times it was undeniable evolution.

One such moment came whilst they were murdering Led Zeppelin's "Black Dog". The band stopped suddenly and Clipper looked over at Egg and smiled broadly.

"For you, this must be like Lionel Messi playing for Cambridge United!"

Egg had gazed at Clipper in confusion. Only when he got

home and googled Lionel Messi did he understand it was meant as a compliment. He realised at that moment, in Clipper, he had the makings of an ally.

Bex always showed up to rehearsals. After one month Egg was able to face her. Two, he could make eye contact. Three, he could hold a conversation. He felt the room light up when she walked in; and he swore, when she greeted them, she would smile at him the longest. The only thing Egg knew of Bex, before being in the band, was that she was beautiful – now he knew she was droll, sharp and even, he thought, remarkable. She spent much of her time taking the piss out of Burt, also something that appealed to him immensely.

As time passed Egg was given increased musical control. He discovered that with the support of Clipper he was able, little by little, to dictate what they would do in rehearsals. It went unspoken, but Egg's musical ability was undeniable. There wasn't exactly gratitude when he taught them something new, but they did listen. With Egg taking control the band's proficiency accelerated and gradually the practice meant more than a twice-weekly excuse to hang out with Bex. The band had grown stronger as a unit and Egg began to enjoy the music. A few months later the band had a solid handle on at least seven cover songs.

Burt – 4th December
Ego is what he should be called, bossing us about
like we're the ones with the style lobotomy.
I chatted with Clipper about it but he hadn't

34

even noticed. So I googled "secret bossiness" and found an expression called "passive aggressive". It means when someone is messin' with your shizzle but you don't know they are. Exactly what Egg the voodoo child is doing. #passiveaggressiveomelette At least the music sounds the business I suppose.

I also blame Ego Egg for me still not pulling Bex. She always sits near him in rehearsal, nodding her fit face and smiling at everyone, except me. I think she's another passive aggressive. I've asked myself the question… Why is she smiling at everyone apart from me? Maybe coz she's uncomfortable with the feelings she has for me? But then I think maybe she lied about liking me if I was in a rock band, because I am actually in a rock band and whenever I sing into her face she just looks at the floor. If she would just look up, I would definitely sing her into a sexual frenzy. I think the turning point is gonna be when she sees me up on stage. No way she'll be able to resist that kind of power.

I'm gonna work stuff out over the holidays.

On a freezing cold January evening the band arrived at rehearsal. It was the first practice for a month.

Tea's noodling irritated Burt almost immediately.

"Can you shut up and stop playing when we're talking?" Burt said. "How we gonna get better if we can't hear ourselves think?"

Tea ignored him.

"Why do you have to play through everything anyway? We're trying to work something out!" Tea looked up, winked at the singer and carried on playing.

"You really are a right proper idiot!" Burt hissed, his face colouring.

"You're the idiot, Burk. Have you considered that I'm trying to work something out for the good of the song?"

"Well can you work it out when we've worked this out!"

"How about I play quietly? Compromise!"

"No! Just shut up!"

Tea stopped noodling and stood up. "I'm off, no point in sitting round here getting verbally abused."

Egg looked at Clipper. Clipper looked at Burt. Tea scowled at all of them. Burt looked worried. "It's not that we don't appreciate you needing time to work stuff out. It's just that it makes things easier to work stuff out without background noise," Egg reasoned softly.

"So I'm background noise, am I?"

"I didn't mean it like that."

"Bollocks to you all, you bunch of tit bandits." Tea put his bass guitar down and began to pack his stuff away.

"Come on, mate! No need to go off in a huff," Burt said.

"For your information I'm not in a huff, I am officially leaving the band … for good!"

"I think we should be an original band," Egg said, out of the blue.

Tea stopped packing his stuff away and stared at the guitarist.

"What do you mean 'original'? We are original," Clipper said puzzled.

Egg shifted in his chair. "Original as in, we write our own songs. It's tedious just playing covers! No wonder we're arguing. Writing our own stuff will be more challenging." Egg looked around the room, expecting a backlash. When none came he continued, "I think it'd be good for us. I think we have a lot to learn. You know – about being in a band. We need to listen to one another for a start."

"Who's going to write the songs?" Tea asked.

"I could have a go, I suppose," Egg said quietly.

"Are you actually mental?" Tea said. "Why would we wanna play one of your songs?"

"Hold on!" Clipper bellowed, putting his hands up. "Have you got something you can play us, Egg?"

Egg nodded slowly, already starting to blush. "It's only rough and I'm not saying that we should play this type of stuff." He paused. "I mean, it's only an idea and…"

"Just play the song!" Tea yelled.

Egg walked over to the school's battered old upright piano and sat down. He closed his eyes and began to play a melancholic tune. Awkward embarrassment spread across his screwed-up face as he began to sing. Clipper let out an audible gasp of surprise. After three-and-a-half minutes Egg finished. The room was silent.

Suddenly the large oak double doors burst open. Bex strode in, made straight for Egg, kissed him full on the lips, pulled back, put her hands on her hips and stared at him.

"That was the most beautiful and awesome-ist thing I have *ever* heard." She paused. "You got any more?"

Egg's face reached new levels of red as he tried to comprehend the delight in her eyes, directed firmly at him. He nodded.

Clipper began to clap. "Bloody brilliant, Egg," he shouted, a broad grin on his face. Tea and Burt were still sitting in stunned silence.

"That wasn't half bad," Tea conceded with a wry smile.

"What are you kissing *him* for?" Burt demanded, staring at Bex angrily.

"You really are an idiot, Burt," she said, rounding on him. "You've been working with Egg for six months, and you've only just discovered that he has the voice of an angel and writes great songs."

"Yeah, but no need to *kiss* him!"

Bex sighed deeply and turned back to Egg. "Have you got more?"

Egg nodded.

"What was that one called?"

"'Satellites'."

"It was really lovely, you really do have a great voice," Bex said softly, sitting down on her usual chair, between Clipper and Egg.

"Your voice is pretty good, even though you sound like a girl," Tea said. "And we don't need no Yoko Ono coming in and spoiling our band dynamic."

"Don't be an idiot, Tea," Clipper said, staring him down. "What band dynamic? Bex is right. For months I've sat on this drum stool and worked on the same old boring songs, listening to you and Burt bitching about how many notes you play. That was the first time I've been totally excited."

Burt looked terrified.

"OK, so Egg can write the songs, but I'm still the singer!" he squirmed, staring around nervously. "Egg has no charisma. He can't be the singer."

Everybody stared back at him in silence.

Egg – 30th January

I played "Satellites" to the band tonight. Bex was listening outside and burst in and actually kissed me and told me she loved it. It was an incredible feeling being kissed like that. She was so excited. It's been decided that I will write the songs but Burt will sing them. To be honest his voice has turned out pretty good. I think it's a little better suited to rock than mine. It's definitely way better than when I first heard it. I'm excited. I told my dad about it all and he said that the last six months might have been tough but it would act as a good foundation for the "new" original band. He's right, as usual. Mum was unsupportive to say the least. She's terrified I will get into drugs, fail my exams and give up my classical music lessons. I told her that the lads think it's posh and stupid doing classical music lessons. She was horrified. I feel a maternal storm coming.

Tea and Clipper easily persuaded their parents to let them practice three times a week. Burt didn't ask; his mum was in Milan and his dad New York. Egg knew he was going to have a problem.

"Please. This is everything I've ever wanted to do," he explained, perched on the edge of the sitting room sofa. His dad sat slumped in the armchair opposite, looking exhausted, whilst his mum stood over him, her arms folded, a deep scowl on her pale face, her mop of thick carroty hair looking crazy.

"What about your school work? Not to mention the years of classical training you're giving up on this … this … whim," she said coldly.

"It's not a whim, Mum, we're getting really good. Anyway, I got straight As in my mocks." He searched his dad's face with pleading eyes. "I'm grade eight in every instrument I play. I'm better than the teachers that tutor me. I promise it won't interfere with how I do in the real exams."

His dad cleared his throat. "OK, look. Here is what we are going to do," he said. "Egg, you can do the band on two conditions."

"Are you undermining me, Tony?"

"I'll do anything," Egg pleaded.

Tony stood up and squeezed his wife's arm. "It's, OK Carol, I think I have the solution."

"I hope so, Tony, I really do."

"If you get those A's you promised us and keep up with at least one of your classical lessons, you can practice three times a week with your band. But if for any reason you let me down on this, you will have to give up the band. Do I make myself clear?"

Egg nodded frantically.

Carol fixed her son a hard stare. "If I see this band affecting you or your behaviour in any way it's over! Do *I* make *my*self clear?"

Egg grinned, barely able to contain his excitement.

Clipper – 6th March

I've decided to start a blog! I got into Charlton Youth today. I'm sixteen in three weeks. Egg told me I'm getting better on the drums. I love the band! Egg's songs are wicked. Tea has started to calm his noodling down. I think we're proper improving. Dad is excited about me doing the band, as long as it doesn't get in the way of football. I have football Saturday, Sunday. Training on Monday and Tuesday and the rest of the week we rehearse. It's well busy, but I love it.

Egg – 8th March

Rehearsals have gone from being the highlight of my week to the only thing I live for. My life has new depths I could only have dreamt about before. It sounds pretentious but the songwriting has become my total focal point. I am almost fanatical about The RockAteers. I work really hard on the songs. I think about everything, even how they will sit together on an album. I present the new compositions to the band like gleaming treasures. Not only do I work on writing the songs, but I iron out the kinks,

make lists of ways the band can improve them and
even write complementary musical parts for the
other instruments.

I'm so glad I encouraged them to rehearse three
times a week because it's making a massive
difference. My classical training has become a
crucial part of the band's new sound, and now they
trust me we are really starting to fly. A couple
of months from the day I played "Satellites" and
we have turned from a pub covers group into a
polished original rock band. It's unbelievable
what you can achieve if you work at it.

Egg had a bounce to his step as he walked back to school for
rehearsal. He had written a new song he thought the band would
like. For no particular reason he took the longer route through
Greenwich Park, up over the hill and past High Bench. The sun
was still shining brightly in the clear spring sky and Egg wondered if he might actually be happy.

He knew something was up as soon as he walked into the
dining hall and was greeted by Burt's beaming face. Burt never
smiled at him intentionally. His band mates were set up and
ready to play. Egg had got into the habit of turning up slightly
late because he could set up faster. Before he could take another
step into the room Burt stood up excitedly.

"I've booked us our first gig!" he announced looking eagerly
from face to face.

Egg stood still, unable to move from the entrance, trying desperately to hide his disappointment.

"That's wicked, mate. Where at?" Clipper responded breathlessly.

"In my garage," Burt proclaimed proudly. "It will be a joint gig and sixteenth birthday I never had!"

"We're not ready!" Egg said, frowning. "I mean we only have a few songs…" He paused. "I actually brought a new song in to play you tonight."

"We need a demo before we do a gig!" Tea said. "How about you pay for it Burt? With all your millions!"

"You know what it means?" Burt said, ignoring Tea and turning to Clipper.

"No? What does it mean?"

"We need to choose a name!" he announced. "Any suggestions?"

Egg shook his head, made his way over to his amp and started to set up his equipment.

"I thought we were called The RockAteers with a capital A," Tea said.

"Temporarily!" Burt replied. "It's not as if any of you like the name, do you?"

"What about Bed Head then?" Tea fired.

"Too sleepy."

"What about Side Winder then?" Tea tried.

"Nah. Been done."

"Who by?" Tea asked.

"I don't know, but I know it's been done," Burt replied, dismissing the idea.

"OK then, how about London Scum?" Tea suggested.

"How we gonna get into the charts with a name like that, Tea?" Burt said. "Be sensible, will you?"

"It worked for the Sex Pistols," Tea replied.

"Can't you take it seriously?" said Burt. "Or shut up."

"Well, if you're gonna speak to me like that…" Tea stood up and unplugged his amp. "Remember the promise you made?" Clipper said forcefully.

"What was that?"

"I agree with Tea. I think it's a lot more important we make a demo than start doing gigs," Egg put in.

"You promised not to strop off all the time," Burt said ignoring Egg. "We had a band meeting last week about it, remember?"

"Yeah, yeah, I know about the rule," said Tea. "Just don't tell me to shut up or I'll be making up my own rules. You get me?"

"How about The Rastafarians?" Clipper said, trying to draw the conversation back.

"That's actually not too bad. What do you think?" Burt asked, turning to Tea.

"What do I think? I think none of us are Rastafarians or even black, Burt," Tea said. "That's what I think."

"You're mixed race!" Clipper said.

"Are you actually mental?" Tea replied.

"Constructive!" Burt added."

"Weapon!"

"What is your problem?"

"Bell-end!"

"You're such a lunatic, Tea!" Burt threw up his arms in despair.

Suddenly the room was filled with the piercing sound of Clipper smashing his sticks down on his snare drum. "Lads! Can't we get on with each other for longer than five minutes?" His band mates stared at him.

"OK then. How about The Love?" Tea suggested.

"Been done before," said Egg, deflated, unable to mask the disappointment of not getting to play his new song. "A band in the sixties from the West Coast of America. They were huge."

"Egg!" Burt snapped. "We don't need a history lesson."

"I really like The Love. Who cares about some old band I've never heard?" Tea said.

"What are you talking about? It's a rubbish name. We'd sound like a girl band."

"OK then, how about the Funky Love?"

"Yeah, the Funky Love Kids." Clipper said.

"That's *it* lads!" Burt stood up. "The Funky Love Children," he announced. "That's proper brilliant!"

SONG 4 HUMILIATION

Sir Wilson Cloom sat and gazed at the multitude of platinum disks hanging from his office wall. What should his next move be? What could a guy who had achieved everything come up with next? He frowned and hit the intercom button.

"Sophia, get Billy Visconti for me right away. If he's not in here in five minutes, you're both fired."

Three minutes later Wilson's intercom buzzed.

"I have Visconti waiting, Sir."

Cloom liked Visconti; not as a person but as a tenacious terrier who got the job done and, more importantly, made him money. If there was one individual Wilson could see taking over his musical empire it was Visconti. Cloom was only fifty-five so he would have to wait at least a decade.

Visconti gave Cloom a confident smile and a double thumbs-up before sitting down in the chair opposite.

"Don't do that, Billy. Neither of us are children and you're not Paul McCartney," Cloom said dourly.

"Message received loud and clear, boss," Billy replied.

Cloom studied the boy. Clean cut, smart, good-looking, with brains. All that helped, but it was Visconti's nose for talent that was the key to his rise. The nose was the most important thing

Cloom looked for in his A&R employees. If they didn't have the nose for a hit then they were no good to him. Billy had the nose of an anteater. He could smell a hit from a hundred miles away.

Things were very different when Cloom had started in A&R. There was no Internet and there were no reality TV shows. It was all about having your ear to the ground and attending as many gigs as it took to discover a star. One thing remained a constant, though. A great song was a great song. If an A&R man could match a charismatic pop act and a great song they were halfway there.

After only three years with Big Tone Records Visconti had sourced and developed three number-one selling acts. Cloom's label had made a lot of money out of that anteater nose. Visconti's talent-spotting abilities were exactly the reason Cloom had made him head of his A&R department. It was also the reason he had sent for him.

"Have we ever signed a rock band, Billy?" he asked, leaning back on his chair.

Billy frowned. "No we haven't, chief."

"Why not?"

"Always more than one ego to deal with, they insist on writing their own songs and don't cross the pond very well, not as much money to be made. You go for mass market, boss. You've always said bands are a headache, that the control you have over artists is the key."

Cloom gave a dismissive wave. "Have you heard this band Desert Kings?" he asked. "Their debut album has sold through the roof."

"Fourth album, boss!" Billy corrected, nodding. "If you're

talking about the big international seller then it would be the Desert Kings' fourth album."

"Don't quibble. I need action," Cloom said, raising his voice in annoyance. "We need to review our attitude towards rock. We need to be part of it." He paused for a moment. "I realise what I have said in the past but I've changed my mind. I can't ignore the sales figures!"

Billy stroked his smooth hairless chin. "I like it, gaffer. We turn one of our developing acts into a rock band?"

"No!" Cloom said. "I mean find me a bunch of kids that write their own songs and play their own instruments. I want them to look amazing and have the kind of angle those Desert Kings guys have. A band that can take America." He paused. "You know they're five sons of a preacher man? I want you to find me a band that has a better angle than that!"

"Three are brothers, Sir. The other two are a brother and sister. The girl, she's the drummer; you could be forgiven for thinking she's a brother."

"Just get it done. Find me the new Desert Kings. You have a month!"

Billy nodded curtly and left the office.

Egg – 1st April
I calculated we were called The Funky Love Children for seventeen hours and twelve minutes. Apparently Bex told Burt that it was the worst name in the history of names and that if we were called The Funky Love Children then she wouldn't

come to the gig. I've never seen a person turn
on his own idea so quickly in my life.

Paul Simon once said: "Improvisation is too good
to leave to chance".

If I could have a quote that people remembered
me for it would be: "Choosing a band name is very
hard".

I don't think we should be doing a gig, but
as a democracy (which I don't think works in
a band) we voted three votes to one in favour.
One good thing is that Bex wants to be our
image consultant and is taking me out to do some
shopping. Spending a full day with her is going
to be amazing. The RockAteers??? We sound like an
adventure film from the 1980s!!!! I think I prefer
The Funky Love Children but Princess Bex has
spoken and I'm not going to argue with her.

Now Burt has started telling us that we all need
to dress the same and that because his style was
the coolest we should all copy him. Tea told him
to piss right off.

The RockAteers were nervous. Burt had opened his house at
noon. Since then a steady stream of schoolmates and strangers
had come in and infested nearly every corner of the house. He'd
invited a couple of local press guys and was thrilled when they
showed up with half an hour to go. Burt wasn't ready to answer

the kind of questions they were asking. "How long are you playing for?", "What are your influences?", "Are you making an album?". The band retreated upstairs and holed themselves up in the music room.

"I can hear everyone outside. It's terrifying." Clipper said, sitting hunched on the piano stool with his back to the keys.

Since arriving, the drummer had spent most of the time in the toilet.

"I'm not nervous!" Burt announced.

"You are nervous, Burt. You've hardly said a word since we've been up here." Tea ribbed. "Why are we all in here again?"

"Because, Tea, bands don't just mill around with their fans, they appear on stage as if by magic and then rock the shiz out of everyone."

Clipper stood up and lurched toward the door. Tea and Burt laughed. Egg continued to stare at the book he was pretending to read.

"Get it all up, Clip, we're on in five minutes!" Burt shouted after him.

A minute later Clipper came back looking sheepish and pale.

"OK guys, let's give the fans what they came for," Burt shouted, startling Egg.

He stood up and waved his hands about for everyone to join him in a group hug.

"I don't think this is necessary, is it?" Tea complained.

"Jesus, Tea, this is what bands do. They have a ritual. It's all about unifying us before we go and rock the shiz out of everyone."

"If you say 'rock the shiz out of everyone' one more time I'm going to shizzle dizzle on your face," Tea said, joining his band mates in an awkward bundle.

"Dear God of Rock, please give us the strength to rock hard. Amen," Burt whispered loudly before breaking the circle.

The band traipsed down the stairs, arrived in the hall and stared around.

"Where have they all gone?" Clipper gulped.

"They must have entered the venue already!" Burt said excitedly.

"It's your garage, Burt!" Tea said, shaking his head in despair.

Sure enough Burt's enormous garage was heaving. The band snaked their way through the jam-packed space, heads down, collecting encouraging pats as they went. A cheer went up as they stepped onto the makeshift stage.

Egg had spent all day setting the equipment up, the school's PA had never sounded so good. Despite being ready to go it took a while for the band to settle. The expectant crowd talked loudly, bristling with anticipation.

Suddenly Burt grabbed the microphone.

"Hello everyone." The place erupted. Burt was briefly surprised before smiling broadly. "Wow, you lot are really all here. Welcome. You're amazing!" Another huge cheer from the hundred-strong crowd.

Burt turned and winked at his band mates. Clipper, his eyes rabbit-in-the-headlights wide, clicked his drum sticks four times and The RockAteers crashed into their opening song, "Bet On You". The garage went crazy. Burt whirled like a madman, pausing to assume every conceivable rock shape known to man. The crowd cheered wildly in response. His guttural drawl was tuneful and edgy. He stopped to stick his tongue out at a pretty looking blonde girl in the front row and glanced at Bex, who was leaning serenely against the garage wall six rows back, avoiding the growing mosh pit developing in front of the stage. Tea gyrated and flew around the improvised stage as if he were playing Wembley Stadium. Clipper attacked the drums like the great grandson of Keith Moon, pointing his sticks at the audience at every available opportunity, sometimes ignoring the need to keep the beat. Egg stood motionless, his guitar loose in his hands, his playing effortlessly perfect. Tea and Burt threw long black and blonde locks at one another in a relentless head bang. The gig rose and fell. Big, ballsy, ambitious rock numbers and fast-paced pop songs kept the tempo high, the diversity addictive. As Burt introduced the last song the crowd were mesmerised. Egg walked over to the keyboard stand and began to play the opening chords of "Satellites". The throng hushed to appreciate the slower paced ballad. Burt changed gear, his voice powerful but sweeter now, more tender. When Egg strummed the last chord the crowd went ballistic.

"Join us in the house for the party up!" Burt shouted before leaping into the crowd and swimming towards the exit.

The throng spontaneously started to sing a rowdy rendition of "Happy Birthday" to Burt. Clipper climbed up on his drum stool and stood grinning from ear to ear as he conducted the crowd with his drumsticks.

Egg searched for Bex in the sweaty throng and found her smiling at him. His nerves abandoned, he beamed back at her. He knew the gig had been a triumph and for once he was glad to be wrong.

The cheering didn't die down until Clipper had left the stage. Everyone streamed back into the house and gathered in the kitchen and ground-floor hallways. Beers were opened and cigarettes were rolled.

"You're gonna be bigger than the biggest band ever!" George told Burt.

Burt waved the flattery away with an unconvincing hand. In the five minutes since finishing the gig he had received at least one gushing compliment every few seconds.

Egg stood by the fridge keeping a low profile, watching Burt working his way around the room collecting praise with a dazzling smile plastered across his face. No one had approached Egg with any kind words. It was as if he was invisible. He was biding his time before he could say goodbye to Burt and get off home. Whilst he waited he watched Bex as she stood with some of the LBC, smiling and laughing and generally looking sexy.

"I wish I could say hello to you!" he said under his breath.

"What did you say?" Burt said, appearing from nowhere.

Egg whirled around. "Nothing!" he said, already reddening.

"Yes you did, you said, 'I wish I could say hello to you'. Hello to who?"

"No one!"

"You better not be looking at Bex?"

"I wasn't!"

"Good! Coz she's well out of your league. Now come on, you idiot, let me introduce you around." He handed Egg a beer. "Chug on some of that before we go. If anyone needs loosening up, it's you." Egg took a long gulp of beer. Burt put a lazy arm around him. "We rocked it tonight, don't you think?" Egg nodded and followed Burt as he moved toward the LBCs sitting around the dining-table.

"Listen up everyone. This is Egg. He's a bit of a tit-head but he's in the band so pass him a few spliffs and make him feel welcome."

Spencer and Zayn nodded cautiously, looking Egg up and down as if it was the first time they had ever seen him. George gave him the middle finger.

Egg felt the familiar hotness in his cheeks double as he sat down.

"Oi, Smeg, you fool, you look like a beetroot!" George shouted.

"Hi. I'm Olivia, I don't think we've met," a pretty blonde girl said with a smile. "So you're in the band? Were you the one in the background?"

"We've been in English class for three years together," Egg said bluntly.

"Who do you hang about with?" asked Chloe, another long-time classmate.

"I don't really know," he replied.

"How can you not know who you hang about with?" George sneered.

"He hangs around with me and the band," Bex said, sitting down at the circular table. Egg felt exhilarated by her sudden presence.

"Smoke weed, Smeg?" George asked, ignoring Bex.

"All the time," Egg replied defiantly, Bex's backing giving him the courage to lie. Bex put a hand across her face.

"Really?" George smirked. "Who do you get your ganja off?"

Egg thought fast. "My dad smokes weed all the time! I use his."

Egg's dad did smoke marijuana. He had a little potting shed at the end of the garden. Inside was an old beat-up armchair, a little portable radio and a poster of Nick Drake. Squirrelled away under some empty clay pots was a generous block of resin. Daily at around seven o'clock he would inform his wife and son he was going to do some gardening. He would return half an hour later with bloodshot eyes and a thousand-yard stare. Egg discovered his stockpile once. He squidged it around for two days before putting it back, unsmoked.

George studied Egg suspiciously, took a deep lug on his trumpet spliff and exhaled into his face. The blue smoke clung to Eggs's hair. Everyone was giggling apart from Bex.

"Get your laughing gear round that then," George said, passing Egg the cone.

Egg accepted the joint with two hands as if it were a rare artefact. Holding it between his little finger and thumb, he stared it and glanced at Bex.

"You don't have to, Egg," she said.

55

He shook his head and took a feeble toke, sucking the smoke into his mouth before exhaling immediately.

George's cold beady eyes were fixed on Egg. "Take a big hit and hold it down, you fanny."

Determined to go down fighting, Egg returned the spliff to his mouth and drew hard. He felt the smoke catch in the back of his throat and pass into his lungs.

"That's it, Egg, now hold it down!" George said excitedly.

Egg battled to keep the smoke down but air started to escape through his nose. Suddenly he was coughing and spluttering uncontrollably, the remaining smoke billowing out of his mouth and nose.

"Water!" Egg gasped.

Burt and George started to slap his back, huge grins stretched across demonic faces. Bex dashed to the sink. Egg struggled to see who was hitting him so hard his eyes were watering so badly. He desperately wanted them to stop, but he couldn't speak through coughing. Bex handed him water and pushed hair from his damp forehead.

"Stop hitting him!" she shouted.

Scores of people had gathered to admire the spectacle of the incredible spluttering kid. Egg's face was purple now. Bex steadied the cup as he took sips. The coughing started to subside.

"I haven't smoked in a while. I got a bit hooked," he croaked. Bex smiled.

"Have a couple more lugs then," George said sweetly, passing him back the joint.

"Don't, Egg," Bex implored.

"Don't, Egg, your fat ginger head might explode," George mimicked.

Bex stared at George for a few seconds, her eyebrow raised.

"You're such a tosser, George. One of these days you're gonna get yours!"

"Oooooh. I'm scared," George sneered. "Come on, Egg, have another lug. You know you want to."

The room was captivated by the unfolding drama. Egg nodded, glanced shamefaced at Bex and took another lug. Bex shook her head and left the kitchen. Egg was encouraged to take another and another by George and Burt. Finally having avoided further coughing fits, he passed the joint on to Olivia, relieved his ordeal was over. A minute passed before George started jeering, stabbing his finger in the direction of the guitarist.

"Look everyone. Egg's chucked a whitey."

"Damn, Egg, you're white as a sheet. Someone fetch a mirror," Burt said, peering down at Egg. His face was swimming in front of Egg's heavy-lidded eyes.

A mirror was held up in front of him. The image Egg saw staring back was horrifying. All pigmentation had vanished from his face. His acne was pronounced, each pimple distinct on his ghoulish features. He felt sick. He stood up. Too fast, his world began to spin, his guts lurched. He stumbled away, tottering through the throng, out of the kitchen and up the stairs towards the third floor bathroom. Finally he reached sanctuary, knelt down over the toilet and made his offering to the porcelain god. When he was finished he curled himself around the throne and stayed there; unable to move, his head whirling, his guts hurting from the heaving. After a while he heard people outside and Burt entered.

"You OK, Egg?"

Egg mumbled a negative.

"You want me to call you a cab?"

He mumbled another negative. He couldn't afford a cab, and he certainly couldn't let his mum see him in this state. Burt left, Egg crawled over to the door and pulled the lock. He heard voices outside on the landing.

"He's never smoked a spliff in his life. Why you got a lying fool like that in your band?" It was George's voice.

"Egg's all right, just a bit of a plank is all," Burt replied. "We'll probably replace him as soon as we get signed."

"He's not even all that good on guitar anyway. Maybe I should join the band?"

Egg passed out.

Clipper – 6th April

Last night was proper good and an absolute nightmare at the same time. I don't think I will ever be able to go out in public again. I got stuck into the drinking after the show and was feeling pretty drunk. Then George comes up to me and starts saying how cool we were and how we should forget about our battles. Then he offered me some spliff. So, because I'm a bit wavy I take it. It was cool to begin with. He told me he saw me play footie the other day and said I had unbelievable tekkers.

Then like a right proper idiot I put my hand on his hand and told him I thought he was actually quite cool. So then he shouts: "Get off me, you fag! Why you touching my hand for?"

He wasn't really saying it to me; he was saying it to everyone else. I was just stood there absolutely gutted. I couldn't move. Then I left. I barely slept all night. I just don't really know what to do about it.

I hope Egg is OK. The last time I saw him he looked like a ghost and was running to the toilet.

Tea – 6th April
The gig was awesome. Loads of weed, booze and fit birds! Talking of birds, at the gig, right up the front, near the stage, was this quite pretty blonde girl with massive boobs. She was absolutely loving it, going mental the whole way through. I tried to chat her up but all she went on about was Burt. Her name was Hazel. She was a bit special in the head if you ask me. Burt's idiot mates were all standing together at the gig. I still need to find out what LBC stands for. George Graves (tool number one – tries to look like Burt with dodgy dyed hair), Spencer (total nob wearing espadrilles and what looked like a sailor's top), Christian (total rugger head with ruddy cheeks and cropped red trousers to match) and Zayn (hair like Beckham had when I was born, Dad owns a chain of off-licences). They looked like tanned *Twilight* vampires on a men's mag

fashion shoot. I looked about for Clip after the show but he must have gone early. I tried to call him today and his phone was switched off which is a bit weird. Egg got well mashed apparently. I didn't see him after the gig as I was talking to Bex in Burt's bedroom. She is bang tidy and dead funny. I really like her, she's cool.

I wish I'd seen Egg chuck a whitey.

Burt - 6th April
Gig was totes amazing. I definitely won man of the match. I was on fire. The flange up the front was weeping for my love pony. I think even Bex was lovin it big style, although she left early because of George. This bird Hazel stared at me the whole way through but I wasn't put off. I suppose I better get used to the fans adoring me up on stage. After the gig, Tea came up to me and told me some girl was well hot for me, so I looked over and it was the same girl, Hazel, who was eyeballing me in the gig. If she tidied herself up she would be quite fit. After Tea pointed her out I noticed that every time I turned round she was there, staring at me. It was like having a stalker. I joked with George that she should be called Crazel not Hazel.

When I crashed out last night at about 3 am Crazel was in my bloody bed. I was sooo wasted and she was really naked so I thought why not! She actually has a pretty nice body but I never should have done it. She is not that fat. She just has amazingly big bangers and wears the

wrong tops for her size (we talked about it!).
She kept saying that because we were both sixteen
we could get married now. She often made no
sense, but I put up with the crazy talk at first.
After a while I had to ask her to leave because
she was doing my head in. She just wouldn't stop
talking about me and her, then I saw her about an
hour later standing outside my house. It really
freaked me out.

I guess she will have to pass the Millie test.

Tried to phone Egg a couple of times today. What
the bloody hell is he playing at? I want us to
play a gig tomorrow night. George is such a plum.
What he did to Egg was going a bit far, even
though it was hilarious at the time.

Egg woke up in a strange room, in a strange bed. He was feeling only marginally better. As his eyes began to focus he saw a
poster of a teenage pop star with a giant fringe that came right
down past his eyebrows. He had a face like a girl. Someone had
drawn a moustache on him in thick black marker pen. Next to
the vandalized pop sensation was a three-dimensional Star Wars
wall chart. It had to be Millie's room. He looked around and saw
lots of Lego mini-figures and pink and purple things. The clock
radio said 2.30 a.m. He looked down at the floor and his heart
sank, there in a crumpled heap by the bed were the cool new
jeans and shirt he'd borrowed from Burt. He moved his hand

over his naked chest and downwards. No boxers! He lifted the heart-patterned duvet and his fears were confirmed. He had been completely stripped. Egg sprung out of bed, grabbed his clothes and dressed quickly.

He stalked down the stairs and peered round the corner toward the kitchen. The coast was clear but he could hear voices. He waited for an eruption of laughter and made for the front door. He lifted the catch carefully and tugged. No give. He felt his way down and found a Chubb key in the lock, turned it and pulled at the heavy door. It creaked loudly, Egg froze. Nothing. He waited for a few seconds before parting the door from its frame and carefully closing it behind him. He knew the kitchen table had a view of the drive and so he skirted around the thick tall hedge. He moved slowly, feeling his way, keeping the hedge that circled the driveway behind him, sideways like a crab.

Egg made it to the far corner of the hedge and could see the heads of the LBC in the kitchen window, laughing, smoking and drinking. Suddenly, just as he thought he had escaped, the courtyard flooded with bright light. He'd tripped the security lights, and like everything else Burt's family owned, they were top of the range. He froze, his eyes skinned on the kitchen window, desperately hoping they would assume it was a city fox on a night raid. No luck. Drunken faces started to appear at the window. Without properly considering the consequences, Egg dived into the hedge and tried to push through it. The tightly-webbed foliage scratched at his face and clothes. He kicked harder when he heard the front door open.

"I definitely saw someone," he heard George's voice slur, "over by the Lambo."

Egg knew his legs were visible and ploughed on through the hedge.

"You're well mashed," said Burt, his voice equally slurred. "You're seeing things, mate!"

"Shhh… Did you hear that?" George hissed. "Over there!"

Egg pushed, squeezed and scrabbled, his head and shoulders at last bursting out of the bush. With one final effort he pulled himself free, landing in a heap in the neighbours' drive. He crouched low and listened, struggling to keep his breathing under control.

"It must have been a fox," Burt said finally, before they went back inside.

Egg let out a long sigh and continued to squat on the neighbours' drive, trying to comprehend the humiliation he had just endured. Finally he stood up, tripped the neighbours' security lights, sprinted out of the drive and trudged the two miles home. It was 3.30 by the time Egg reached sanctuary. As soon as he opened the front door the hallway flooded with light. His mother was barring his way. Arms crossed and her face full of thunder.

"Egg, where the hell have you been? Why are your clothes wrecked?"

Egg remained silent. His dad appeared from the sitting room, his face tired and concerned.

"Egg," his dad said, staring at his son's hairline in horror. "Where the hell are your eyebrows?"

Egg put hands up to his forehead, his eyes growing wider as he examined himself. He pushed past his parents, bolted upstairs to the bathroom and looked in the mirror.

He had no eyebrows, none at all.

Egg – 6th April

I didn't sleep all night. It gave me a chance to
work out what I was going to do and say about
this tragedy. This morning we had a family
meeting. Mum said I had to leave the band. I told
her I had shaved my own eyebrows off. She knew I
was lying but I didn't care.

Should I leave the band? No, that was exactly
what George wanted. So what! I'd wear a hat for a
few weeks till my eyebrows grew back. Who cares,
at least things were happening, even if some of
it was the stuff of nightmares.

This is an epiphany moment. I can either sink or
swim. I choose to swim.

SONG 5 DEMONSTRATIONS

Tea pulled out the lengthened coat hanger from his jacket, leaned against the car and pushed the rod into the gap between door and window. He jimmied the lock and after a few seconds heard the click. With a quick glance over his shoulder he climbed into the car and began hot-wiring. Moments later the engine roared to life. Tea smiled. Delighted with his own cunning, he put the car in gear and drove the short distance to Burt's house.

Why Burt hadn't just borrowed the money the band needed from Mummy and Daddy was beyond Tea. Burt's house was massive. They had to have millions in the bank. What was a few grand to them? Tea had had enough of car boot sales and car-washing marathons. It was degrading washing other people's cars. All they had raised was seventy-nine quid, not even a tenth of what they needed to get the demos cut at London's famous Dean Street studios. Tea had questioned the need for a demo in the first place, but Burt said that without one there was no way they'd get a record label to a gig and subsequently get signed for a million pounds. Tea had decided to accelerate the progress.

Tea pulled into Burt's driveway and came to a stuttering stop. He left the engine running and got out of the car.

"There's at least four hundred quid," he mumbled happily as he walked around the car, stroking it with his palm.

Burt appeared at the front door of his huge house. "What's that?" he asked, pointing to the car.

He was wearing the most outlandish ensemble Tea had ever seen.

"Is that a crop top?" Tea asked with a frown.

"I'm sunbathing in the garden."

"In women's underwear?"

"It's not women's underwear. These are bullet hole jean shorts from Dolce and Gabbana," he said defensively, "and this T-shirt is Louis Vuitton. Anyway, stop changing the subject… What the hell is *that*?"

"It's music," Tea said, patting the car roof with a proud smile.

Burt walked down the marble steps and cocked his head in confusion. Tea stared in horror at his band mate's feet.

"What are they?"

"You know perfectly well what they are, Tea. They're flip-flops."

"Yeah, but what are they doing on your feet? They look well gay!"

"What do you mean, 'It's music'?" Burt said, ignoring the comment.

"I'm going to sell it and we are going to use the money for the demo." Tea paused. "That's why it's music."

"Where did you get it from?"

"A mate gave it to me."

Before Tea could stop him Burt dashed across the gravel and dived into the car's open door. He righted himself, opened the glove compartment and rifled through the booklets, files and loose papers. Tea looked on in shock.

"D.I. Ramsey?" Burt exclaimed, holding up the piece of paper he had been looking for.

"Yeah, my mate Mrs Ramsey. She's great!" Tea replied, quick as a flash.

"What's her first name?"

Tea looked flummoxed. "Dora," he blurted.

Burt returned the documents to the glove compartment, got out of the car and slammed the door. "Isn't Dora your mum's name?" he asked sternly, stepping into Tea's personal space. "You nicked it!"

"So I nicked it! Who cares? We need a demo more than Dora Ramsey needs a car."

"Take it back!"

"No way!" Tea replied. "I didn't go to all the trouble of nicking it just to take it back. Who died and made you king?"

"Take it back or you're out of the band." Burt took another step forwards, close enough for Tea to get a powerful whiff of cologne. He held his ground, returning the singer's stare defiantly.

"I'm serious, take it back now or you're out of the band!"

Tea broke the stare, exhaled slowly and nodded. "OK, but you better come up with a plan to get the money, Burt. I'm not cleaning no more cars." He turned, got back into the car and drove away, wheel-spinning his way out of the drive.

Tea drove steadily towards the estate, simmering with anger. The band was everything to him. How dare Burt threaten to take it away? What right did he have? Burt would pay for that.

Five minutes of quiet rage passed before he reached the shabby entrance to the estate. He drove up the heavily potholed one-way street. The six-storey, 1950s red-brick flats rose up on either side, suffocating the street below. Tea spotted his uncle standing on his usual corner smoking a joint. Tea tried to duck and hide but it was too late.

Tea loved and respected his Uncle. Frank was the estate's Mr Fix It and he had come in useful on more than one occasion. Not so long ago Tea and his mum had been burgled. The robbers had taken everything of any value from the tiny flat. Tea had gone to see Uncle Frank. He'd gone mental, made one phone call and within half an hour the house contents had been returned to Frank's doorstep.

Uncle Frank stepped into the road and put a hand up. Tea stopped. Frankie the Hat was dressed in his usual black leather knee-length coat, a black shiny shirt and fake alligator cowboy boots, his long greased hair straggling out from under his trademark trilby. Frank got into the passenger side.

"Drive to the garage and don't say a bleeding word."

Tea complied. A minute later he pulled up outside his uncle's heavily graffitied garage.

Frank relit his joint and passed it to his nephew. "Going for a drive, Michael?" he asked.

Tea remained silent.

"What if I told Dora about your flash new motor?" He gave Tea's knee a squeeze until he squirmed in pain. "You reckon she'd be best pleased?"

"I know you've nicked cars, Uncle Frank. Everyone knows you nicked cars and much worse besides."

Frank studied his nephew with cold black eyes. "This ain't what I want for you, boy!" Tea met his serious gaze. "And I bloody well know know it ain't what your mother wants for you neither."

Tea dropped his head. "Unc, I need money. I asked Mum but she didn't have nothin'. So I improvised. I thought you'd be proud of me."

"Proud? Proud you might turn out like that excuse of a father?" he hissed. Tea shrunk back in his seat and Frank's voice softened. "Look, I don't want you to have the life me or your old man have. Always looking over your shoulder. I love you're in this rock band. I want you to have a straight and narrow life. Get out of this dump," he gestured outside.

"I did what I had to. We need dough for a demo. It's going so well, Unc, we've done two gigs round Burt's gaff and we just keep getting better. Everyone's lovin' it large style. We've gotta take the next step."

Frank reached inside the leather jacket and pulled out a thick roll of notes. "How much you need, boy?"

Tea shook his head. "I can't take that money."

"Why not? It wasn't earned fair or square. It either goes on a work of art or half a key of coke. Your choice." Frank grinned.

"Well at least take the motor?"

"Nah, I'll tell you what I'm doing with this. I'm taking it back and putting it exactly where you found it. You've nicked an unsellable!"

"What do you mean?"

"I'm not telling ya. But trust me, trying to sell this would get me nicked."

"Why? You got to tell me."

"Because it's old bill, Michael. You've gone and stolen an unmarked car." Frank let out a snort of laughter before controlling himself and looking back at his distraught nephew.

"I'm an even bigger idiot than my dad," Tea moaned quietly.

"Don't ever say that," Frank said, pulling Tea toward him so he could feel his uncle's stale breath on his face. "You're a much bigger idiot than your old man. He never would have nicked no Babylon car."

Tea smiled broadly and his uncle chuckled. Soon both were in fits of laughter.

Burt – 9th April
Since I've been in the band the fanjeeta is literally attacking me, like an army of rabid beavers. I could have sworn that Bex was gonna love me all night long after my performance on stage the other night. It was so good we did it again on the Sunday night. I had the crowd eating out of my hand. What's the bloody matter with that girl? She should be gagging for it! I was wearing my best clobber. Is she actually a lunatic? #checklisttime

1. I'm the best-looking kid in school.
2. I'm in a rock band (which is exactly what she wanted in the first place).
3. I did an amazing gig that everybody went absolutely mental for.

I had the big talk with Egg the Omelette about

his crap clothes the other week. I'm not going
in to record our first ever demo with a kid that
looks like some kind of Goth Geek hybrid. I know
he writes the songs but he's letting the side
down. I've read all the rock'n'roll books and
seen all the rockumentaries. Bands don't work as
a democracy and I'm the obvious leader.

Rule 1. A band needs an image.
Rule 2. That image needs to be the Desert Kings
image because that's what's in at the moment.

Anyway it backfired coz Bex said that she would
take Egg shopping and they didn't need me to come
– "we'd be more comfortable without you there,"
she said – whatever that's supposed to mean. Now
all I have to do is convince Tea to shed his
rapper's outfit for skinny jeans and cool shoes.
No chance.

I am exasperated about what to do with the demo.
We really need the money. I refuse to ask my folks
like the lads keep suggesting. No way.

Burt let himself in, routinely checked his reflection in the hallway
mirror and made his way to the kitchen. Millie was busy beside
the eight-burner range cooker; her red plastic-framed glasses
steamed up as she opened the oven door.

"Those new frames are cool," Burt said, throwing his car
keys down.

Millie turned and smiled. "Thanks. The blue ones died in an incident involving a skipping rope and a football today. Ten per cent my fault, ninety per cent Stella's."

Burt grinned. "What's for dinner?"

"Ham Tagliatelli from M & S. Get us two plates, will you."

"Yep, any news from the home front?"

"Mum said she will try and come back for a couple of days in a few weeks," she said over her shoulder. "Oh, I found your wallet!"

"Where?"

"On the living-room coffee table in plain view. Only a tool wouldn't have spotted it."

"Hey!" Burt frowned. "Where did you learn that?"

"From you!" she said, grabbing the oven gloves. "I paid Linda. She said you owed her more but I'm sure my maths is right. I was a bit confused."

Burt coughed. "Yeah, yeah. I do owe her, don't worry, I'll sort it."

"I know you pay Linda to roll you spliffs. I'm not dumb."

Millie placed a plate of pasta in front of her brother and joined him at the dining table.

Burt flushed. "How do you know?"

"Your laptop!"

Burt choked on his pasta. "What?"

"You leave your laptop open all the time."

"Mills, that's personal shit in there!" He paused. "It's too old for you. I've told you before!"

Millie shrugged and twizzled a fork full of pasta before letting it all drop onto the plate. "You need money for the demo, don't you? Like, you *really* need money?" Before Burt could say anything she got up from the table, scraped a stool over to the utility shelves and climbed on top. She strained and stretched to reach the uppermost shelf – finally laying her hands on a small biscuit tin, she climbed back down and returned to the table.

"I want you to have it." She handed her brother the colourful container. Burt wanted to laugh.

He opened the tin and almost choked on his mouthful of pasta.

"Where the hell did you get all this money?"

"Been saving it! It's my pocket money," she told him. "Twenty pound a week for nearly two years. I think there's about £700 in there."

"Is that all you get?"

"Yes, I'm nine."

"Well, I can't take this, Mills. It wouldn't be right!"

"Yes it would. What am I going to spend it on? I've got all the Star Wars Lego I need right now. I want you to have it. To do the demo."

Burt studied his sister for a long time before answering. "OK, but I'm going to pay you back ten times over when we are famous."

"Sounds like a plan!"

Egg – 12th April
I'm going on a shopping trip with Bex tomorrow,
just me and her. I cannot wait. I just hope
Burt doesn't turn up and do his usual thing of

letching all over her. I can tell Bex doesn't
like it. Why can't he just get the message? She's
not interested in superficial things like money
and good looks.

"Thing about image is it's totally changeable. Nothing can't get sorted. We can sort out your bowl cut, glasses, spots and dodgy all-black outfit," Bex told Egg as they paced down Oxford Street. "We could even dye your ginger hair. But I don't think you should, coz I like it!"

"What's wrong with all black?"

"Nothing wrong with a bit of black if you're wearing it with style!" she replied before diving into a shop.

Egg was struggling hugely with the reality of being outside school, at a weekend, on a shopping trip, with Bex. He kept wondering whether it was all an elaborate joke; that he would arrive at Oxford Circus tube and find a crowd waiting for him, pointing and laughing, with George screaming "You didn't think this was for real did you!?" But it *was* real and, anyway, Egg trusted Bex. Today they could finally talk, if his nerve held. He could find out about her and they could make a connection. Throughout her time watching them rehearse she had appeared nothing other than genuine. She was everything he'd hoped she would be all those times he'd watched her from across the canteen. Walking next to her, being able to turn and look at her all of the time was incredible; her thick sweet-smelling hair and sparkling green eyes. He felt the heat in his cheeks subside with every minute in her smiling, relaxed company.

Bex flew through the store, flicking at clothes on rails, letting out the occasional tut or picking an item up for a closer look.

"What about this?" she said, holding a jean shirt up against him.

Egg nodded. "As long as it fits in with Burt's image idea."

He glanced around the cool, dark shop with its distinctive smell. It was so alien to him. He wished he had worn cooler clothes, but he didn't have any.

"It fits. Egg, you don't have to do this for the band. You should do it for yourself! Looking good might make you feel happy, and being happy is what it's all about, I reckon."

She shot off between the racks of dark clothes.

"I thought getting married and having kids is what life was all about," Egg replied, as Bex continued collecting items on her crooked arm.

She shot a glance back at him. "Egg! We're fifteen! Right now the meaning of life is having a laugh. You can have kids when you're thirty. You're old before your time," she teased, flashing him a smile. "Right, let's try this gear on?"

She headed for the changing rooms.

The heavily styled gatekeeper had tattoos, a quiff and what Egg considered to be an earnestly affected attitude. He counted the items, passed Bex a plastic card with the number eight on it and gave her an exaggerated wink. Bex ignored him and went up the tunnel.

As Egg passed to follow, the tattooed man looked him up and down, shook his head and kissed his teeth. Before Egg could comprehend the contempt, Bex had rotated 180 degrees and quick-stepped it back up the tunnel, her face stern and determined.

"Did you just kiss your teeth at my friend?" she fired – her words like bullets. She leaned into the shop assistant's face.

"No!" the tattooed man replied, shifting awkwardly on his stool.

"Good! Because kissing your teeth doesn't suit you. You need to learn some manners."

Egg watched as he crumbled before the Bex glare. She turned and strutted back down the tunnel. Egg scuttled after her.

"Right, go in there," she demanded, pointing to one of the changing rooms.

"OK!" Egg answered, moving into the cubicle. Bex followed him in.

"What you doing?" Egg gasped.

"I'm keen to see you naked, Egg!" she replied seriously.

Egg flushed in embarrassment. "Oh, yes. Well I…"

Bex shook her head. "I was joking. I want to see what this stuff looks like on you!" She paused and turned her back to him. "Look, I'll stay with my back to you until you're ready. OK?"

She turned and faced the corner of the booth.

Egg stared at her back in silence for a long moment.

"Did you tell that bloke he shouldn't kiss his teeth because he's white?" Egg eventually asked.

"I didn't say he couldn't kiss his teeth because he's white! I just said it didn't suit him. My dad's Jamaican and when he kisses his teeth you know about it. When that idiot kissed his teeth it sounded as if he was sucking a sweet."

"I thought you were South American?"

"My mother's from Argentina."

"So how come you look more Argentinian than black?"

"Wow, Egg, I don't know, it's just the way it worked out! What does it matter? Just get undressed. We haven't got all day."

Egg flushed and slowly began to unpick his shirt buttons.

"I'm very pale!" Egg warned.

"That's nice," she replied. "I can't see you anyway but I like pale."

"No, I mean it's not a pretty sight."

"Why are you so down on yourself all the time? So what if you've got light skin. You're a wicked person and an amazin' songwriter. Why you gotta think on things that don't matter. I'd rather not be saying this shit stuck in the corner of a changing cubicle, by the way."

He smiled awkwardly. "Why did you stick up for me?"

"Because I'm sick of folk who think they're 'all dat'. What right has he to judge you just coz of the way you look?" She paused. "Look, Egg, I know men look at me, fancy me, whatever and I could probably use that for evil like loads of girls do. But I use my powers to help mankind or … in this case, Egg-kind," she laughed.

Egg laughed too, finally pulling on a pair of slim-fit jeans and slipping a white crew-neck T-shirt over his head. "OK, I'm ready." Bex turned round and Egg gave a gauche twirl.

Was that a hint of surprise in her eyes, he wondered.

"Wow, Egg, looking good. I could actually quite fancy you like that."

The heat returned to Egg's cheeks.

Bex smiled. "Come on, try on the rest. Those are keepers.

"I can't afford even one of these items," Egg replied, inspecting the price tag on the jeans.

"Don't worry," Bex said, sliding a card out from her back pocket, waving it and giving him a mischievous smirk. "I have it covered."

"I can't let you pay for it."

"I'm not. Burt is," she said, holding the card closer to his face.

He read the name on the card. James Burt Windsor. Egg raised his eyebrows and pulled a face to her grin.

"How did you get his card?"

"Getting close to Burt is not a problem I have."

Egg smirked. "But, how did you get his pin number?"

"It's the day and month of his birthdate. He told a whole load of us when we were hanging out by High Bench last summer. I think he was trying to show off but it's beyond me what's impressive about it."

After buying three T-shirts, two pairs of jeans and two pairs of shoes, Bex took Egg to get his hair cut. The transformation complete, the pair wandered through Soho to a little park and sat in the sun chatting. There was an ease between them that Egg could only have dreamed of the evening before. Bex told him everything, from how to look after his skin to who her favourite bands were. It was the best day of Egg's life.

At seven o'clock they walked down to Trafalgar Square and got on the bus back to South London.

"I'll walk you home," Bex said as they got off the number 53.

"Isn't it supposed to be the other way round?" Egg asked.

"I'm not the one with an eight o'clock curfew, Eggsy," she teased.

They walked slowly, chatting and laughing as they strolled through the leafy suburb. At three minutes to eight they reached Egg's small terraced house.

"I want to meet this dragon of a mother of yours," Bex leaned in and whispered. Before Egg could reply she had rushed up to the front door and had rung the bell.

Egg's mother, Carol, answered the door in a brown sack-like dress and reindeer slippers. Egg winced with embarrassment. She looked Bex up and down disapprovingly before letting her glare loose on Egg.

Bex appeared undeterred. "Hello Mrs Poacher, I'm Bex," she said holding out a hand.

Egg stood rooted to the spot, unable to look up from the floor.

"Egg, come inside. You're late." Carol said, ignoring the hand as she studied her son. "What in heaven's name are you wearing?"

"New clothes, Mrs Poacher. He looks great doesn't he?" Bex said brightly, studying her rejected hand as if to see what was wrong with it.

"I better go. See you soon," Egg said as he shuffled past and into the house. Like a human gate, his mother stepped aside to let him through and stepped back quickly to bar the way.

"You should be ashamed of yourself," Carol hissed.

Bex's eyes narrowed in confusion. "I don't understand."

"What are you doing hanging around my son? Is it some kind of dare? Has someone put you up to it?"

Egg wanted to die.

"I don't understand what you mean," he heard Bex respond.

"A girl who looks like you doesn't go around with boys like my son. He was a good boy before he joined the band. He always listened to his mother. You know shaving his eyebrows off is bullying don't you?"

"But I had nothing to do with shaving his eyebrows off and he is my friend. I'm the lucky one. I like your son."

Carol frowned uncertainly, nodded curtly and shut the door.

Egg – 14th April

I'm an emotional yoyo. On the one hand I was overjoyed to spend so much quality time with Bex, and on the other my mum is driving me mental. Whenever I feel like this, I get on the piano or pick up the guitar. I wrote a song called "Shop Till You Drop". No idea where the lyrics came from, LOL. But I think it's got something. I can't wait to play to the band.

Shop Till You Drop

Verse 1
Shop till you drop you can't stop, where you gonna go in your next stop baby?
Heaven won't help, hell won't let you in.

*Stop it, block it, lock it keep it safe away, well you won't last one
single day.*
Heaven won't help, hell won't let you in

Bridge
I can see for miles and miles. Can you? I don't think you do.

Chorus
I can see for miles and miles and miles and miles and miles
Forever you, forever me, forever young, forever free

Tea — 14th April
Uncle Frank gave me a fat grand toward the demo.
It wasn't enough to use the studio we wanted to
use, so Burk told Egg and Clipper to ask their
parents. Egg said his mum and dad were skint and
why didn't Burk ask *his* parents, seeing as they
were millionaires. Burk said that wasn't fair
and it wasn't going to happen. He didn't want
anything from his parents.

Then the next day, Burk suddenly tells us that
his parents have given him £700 in cash. It seems
he does want something from his parents after
all. He's so lame. I still haven't forgiven him
for mugging me off and threatening to throw me
out of the band.

"The vocal needs to be louder," Burt demanded, as The RockAteers sat listening back to the music they had created. The sixteen-person leather sofa that lined the back of the room faced a long, deep control desk and a bank of computer screens. Clipper said it looked like a spaceship. The control desk, with all its faders, backlit buttons and knobs faced a thick double-glazed window. Through the window lay the huge live space. "That's where the magic happens," said Burt. The sound engineer thought differently.

The RockAteers had been in London's Dean Street studios for five days straight, ten hours a day. The boys had never worked harder during a school holiday in their lives. Egg was feeling the pressure. He worked obsessively on making the demo perfect during the day and then spent most of the night revising. The band had chosen three songs: "Love and War" – a rousing, ambitious track Egg had written about Bex; "Golden" – a rousing, ambitious track Egg had written about Bex; and "Satellites" – a rousing, ambitious track Egg had written about Bex.

"It's natural for you to want to hear more of yourself," the sound engineer, Toby, explained to Burt. "But it isn't always what's right for the overall mix."

The lack of space and light in the basement was an alien and uncomfortable environment for the band. Now cabin fever and little sleep combined with Burt's constant manic talking was driving everyone crazy, Toby included.

"What a surprise. Big-head Burk wants to be turned up!" Tea commented, making Clipper laugh.

Burt was not amused. "I read on the Internet," he said loftily, "that the vocal is eighty per cent of what people listen to in any song! So I'm not big-headed, it's for the good of the band."

"You *are* big-headed, Burt," Tea said. "I've never known anyone with a bigger head."

Toby raised his hands. "Guys, all this banter is really slowing things up. It's not productive."

The RockAteers fell silent.

After five minutes the arguments flared up again and Toby reached his limit. "Look lads, I think this would be a lot quicker if you left me to it."

"Come on," said Egg, standing up. "You heard him. Let's go out for a bit."

Egg had been there for every moment of the track-laying and was quietly happy with the results. The songs sounded pretty much as he had hoped. He had worked with each of his band mates to get their best performance, and the effort had been rewarded. "Satellites", the first song he had ever played to the band, had received special praise.

"Loads of bands would kill for a song like this," Toby said. "It's got hit written all over it."

Lucy, the studio manager, also loved the songs.

"Tea or coffee?" The assistant engineer, Ollie, asked every half an hour. "Anything from the shop?"

Egg was uncomfortable with Ollie doing whatever the band asked of him. Burt found it less difficult to adjust, Ollie quickly becoming the singer's personal slave. On day three Egg suggested he tone it down.

"We gotta get our money's worth," Burt replied.

Egg shook his head and gave up.

"How did you convince your parents to give you the money for this place?"

"Told 'em I'd pass my exams."

Words failed Egg. There was no way that was going to happen, but from what Egg had gathered, Burt's parents wouldn't know or care.

Clipper – 17th April
I played my dad the rough versions of the tunes and he loved them. He went right proper mental for "Bet On You" and said that "the metaphorical nature of the song was well clever" and that the big production suited the songs brilliant. His accent went all posh when he said it. I think he misses being in the music industry, he was a mobile disc jockey in his twenties. Can't wait to tell Egg my dad thinks the song is right proper metaphorical.

I reckon he got more out of loving the songs than when he sees me play football, or maybe that's just me wishing. He told me all this stuff about when he was younger he put on Northern soul nights. We talked for ages. He was really digging it. I think it's the first time he's ever been proud of me for anything other than football. He said as long as I don't let it interrupt things when I go to Charlton FC in a few months he would support me doing the band stuff.

I'm worried that in the end I might have to choose between football and music. I think I know what I'd choose. I've not played FIFA for months now either. I don't even see the point in studying for my exams. I'm not cut out for being educated.

I'm sixteen tomorrow and free to make my own decisions. I have to give my answer to Charlton Athletic youth team soon. My dad knows everything about football and that's why he has kept me out of any big youth teams till now. I think it's amazing because he's obsessed by football but he still wanted me to experience other things first. The fact that he's a huge Charlton fan worries me even more. He reckons I would get in the U18's first team pretty quick even though I'm only nearly sixteen. I just don't want to let him down. He is so excited about it all. There's some other stuff I could do with asking my dad about, but I'm pretty sure he wouldn't understand.

Bex arrived at Dean Street studios on the third day of recording with a professional-looking camera bag slung over her shoulder and a huge leather case with wheels and a handle. Within ten minutes she had charmed everyone who worked there. The older girls that managed the space were enchanted and the male producers and engineers spellbound.

Burt was all over her as soon as she arrived. Egg loved to watch his lead singer being shot down. Bex was so good at it.

She was great mates with both Tea and Clipper, but as much as Burt tried, he never seemed to get her approval. Egg decided that if there was a fifth member of The RockAteers it was her. She was never unwelcome. Not even by Burt, despite the torrid time she gave him.

"I've brought my camera, lads!" she declared, as they took a break from recording and sat in the luxurious lounge.

"What for?" Burt griped, still smarting from the put-down she had given him upon arriving.

"I thought I could take some band shots. If you're making a demo then you're gonna want to put some tunes up online, so you need visuals, right?"

"We got someone lined up, thanks!" Burt told her.

"No we haven't, Burk of Burk Hall!" Tea snarled, turning to Bex. "Pictures would be wicked, darlin'. Where do we sign?"

Egg shifted in his seat. Bex grinned at him. "I brought a ton of clothes for you all to try," she said, patting the suitcase. "We need to get you all looking like you're in the same band. I also brought some hair product and a bit of foundation to stop facial shine!"

"I'm not wearing no make-up!" Burt said.

Bex rolled her eyes. "Fine, Burt, your face can be all shiny. You like standing out anyway, so that's cool."

Burt looked bewildered.

"I've talked to Lucy and she will let us use Studio 3 to change in," Bex said, passing Clipper the huge leather bag.

"Whose is all this clobber?" Clipper asked.

"I borrowed it off my brother. He's at Fashion College."

Clipper's eyes widened. "Oh wow, I didn't know that! So what's the style?"

Bex looked thoughtful. "I reckon use what Burt is wearing as a template. You want a look that's accessible and unique. If we can get everyone looking a bit like him then I think we can achieve a unified image. Pretty sure the stuff in the bag will do the job."

"See!" Burt growled. "How long have I been telling you bunch of losers to start taking this image thing seriously? How long have I been saying that I should be the one you all copy?"

Tea stood up and shook his head. "Burt, you really have no idea what an absolute nob you are, do you?" he said before disappearing towards Studio Three.

Burt gave Tea's back the finger and rose to follow with Clipper and Egg.

"Egg, can I have a quick word?" Bex asked.

"What you want a word with him for?" said Burt.

"None of your business, Burt. You're such a paranoid freak."

Burt looked from Bex to Egg and back again before retreating up the corridor.

"How's things with your mum?" she asked when they were alone.

Egg shrugged.

"All right I suppose. She's still dead against me being in the band, but as long as my marks are good," he paused. "I'm her only kid and she thinks I should be a classical musician. She always wanted me to do something creative and she thinks all this rock stuff is a waste of my infinite talent." Egg grinned at her bashfully.

"I wish you could look at me for longer than five seconds, Egg. You've got well beautiful eyes, you know."

Egg dropped his gaze and blushed.

"I want you to wear the stuff I put in the white plastic bag inside the big leather one. You get me?"

"Is it a monkey suit?"

Bex giggled.

Suddenly Egg stopped smiling and fixed Bex with steady look. "Bex… I wondered if you might fancy… I mean if you're not doing anything else, well … if we might…"

"Smeg, come on you long streak of piss! We have a photo shoot to smash and you're the worst-dressed person in Europe," Burt shouted, leaning around the door with a scowl.

Egg got up and slouched out of the room.

SONG 6 NETWORKING

Egg – 21st April
Bill Gates once said: "Be nice to nerds. Chances are you'll end up working for one."

That's all very well, Bill, but why am I the one doing all the work? I've just spent all night setting up the Twitter, YouTube and FaceBook pages for The RockAteers. I thought getting all A's in my mocks would keep the heat off from Mum, but now she says I won't be allowed to do anything with the band unless I show her evidence of studying hard for the real ones. I wish I was sixteen like the rest of the lads. It sucks being the youngest in my year. If I was sixteen I could do whatever I liked.

The songs take ages to upload on my mum's ancient computer. I should have gone round to Burt's. He has a whole room dedicated to computers but I couldn't take another hour with him at the moment. The days at the studio were quite harrowing. I don't think I realised the full extent of his out-of-control ego. Anyway the songs sound amazing so it's not all bad. Bex came down to the studio on the last day and she was really complimentary. She said that we were going to be huge stars and that the tunes sounded much bigger and more American than she had expected.

I took that to mean we could be big in the US. A
good thing, I think. Burt was all over her like
a rash. I got this horrible feeling suddenly that
she secretly quite likes it. Could that be true?
It did my head in thinking of those two together.

Lucy, the manager of Dean Street Studios, said that
she had never heard such an accomplished young band
with such a great bunch of songs. She was the one
that suggested the strings and arranged a string
quartet to come in. All for free. It was great
writing string parts, I've never done that before
(I hope they sound OK). Toby, the sound engineer
said he would work with us anytime. Is it wrong
to like Toby more than my own band mates? Except
Clipper of course, who is pure brilliance.

I was so close to asking Bex out but then Burt
burst in and ruined it all. She took some band
shots with her dad's big digital camera whilst
we were in Soho. She sorted me out stuff to wear
and I think I actually looked all right. She had
already scoped out this really cool derelict area
down an alley way for the photo shoot. Burt kept
trying to say that he should be up the front or
in the middle but Bex kept replying that she was
taking the photos and he needed to do as he was
told. Me, Tea and Clipper loved it. She kept
leaning into us wearing this low-cut top. She is
just so unbelievably hot. The photos are pretty
amazing, really edgy and cool. I have to hand it
to Burt for getting Tea out of his baggies and
into some rock'n'roll gear. We do look like a
band now. We look like the Desert Kings on acid.
The pics look good on Facebook etc. Just waiting
for the bastard songs to upload now. Thing is I
can't stop listening to them.

Tea – 21st April

Burt has forced the band to wear exactly the
same clothes. What sixteen-year-old wears leather
shoes when he doesn't need to? He keeps going
on about this band The Desert Kings. I googled
them the other day and they all look well proper
stupid. The lead singer actually looks like he's
wearing girls' leggings. Skinny jeans is one
thing, but not if they look like they've been
painted on. Anyway I'm sick of arguing about it.
What a load of bollocks. I've surrendered. Burt
has worn me down and I will admit the ladies like
my new look. The new demo sounds proper wicked
though, so it's all good. I must have played "Bet
On You" a million times. Bex took a bunch of pics
of us for the Internet sites. God she's fit. She's
like a cross between Rihanna and Ariana Grande.
She is also the coolest bird I ever did meet.

Burt – 22nd April

I shouldn't have let Egg do the Facebook, what
an imbecilic fool. He chose the one picture of me
looking well dodgy for the profile. Also everyone
knows the lead singer should be up the front in
photos. What's his game? What was Bex playing
at?! She was the one that insisted we share the
limelight.

The tunes sound deadly though and my voice is
amazing. I nailed it. We already have 4,500 likes
on Facebook and even more on Twitter. How did

that happen? I told a few lads at school and now everyone shouts "RockAteers" when I walk past. It's like we're famous or something. Crazel actually sung the whole of "Satellites" back to me in the corridor at school yesterday. I've known her since primary school apparently. She's got big tits but they're nowhere near as nice as Bex's. She told me that she's our uber fan. That weirded me right out. The girl won't leave me alone.

Bex hasn't personally told me she loves the music. Not even once. She's complimented Egg loads. Like I'm bothered, I've got my pick of every fit girl in school now (not that I didn't before). Problem is I can't stop thinking about her. I'm not jealous of an idiot like Egg, but I think I might start acting like him for a bit. You know, like all understated and stuff. Maybe Bex will like me more if I do some of that. Maybe the combo of my devastating good looks, cool clothes, massive shlong and Egg's boring personality is what she wants. Worth a try!

Booked a gig for us today. It's a battle of the bands and if we win we get dollars. It's in a month. Reckon we can sell some CDs as well.

Social networking sites were Billy Visconti's speciality. It didn't strike him as odd that his job required him to spend half his working week searching for talent on the Internet. Or that he had thousands of cyber-friends, most of whom he had never even met.

When it came to his popularity on the web Billy was realistic. He knew that his connection to Sir Wilson Cloom and the work he did was the major reason he was so well-liked in the virtual world. He also knew that his boss's generation still found social networking something to distrust. The old industry execs who didn't embrace the changes were doomed. Billy couldn't wait for the dinosaurs to move over.

Billy had ways of knowing when the kids were being drawn to something on the web. Specially designed computer programmes alerted him when something online was getting a lot of heat. He had been all over the Justin Bieber Youtube thing way back when he was only an intern, but had lost out on signing him because Wilson had dismissed the buzz as a flash in the pan. Billy was determined never to miss out again. He needed to jump on things sooner. He had to be more insistent with his boss.

Missing out on Bieber wasn't all bad. When Wilson saw the teen heart throb selling millions of records he promoted Billy. It was Cloom's way of owning up to the mistake. Billy's ambition reached new heights.

Despite having every scout and Facebook ally primed and looking out for the younger English version of the Desert Kings, Billy had unearthed nothing and he was starting to get nervous. Cloom was an impatient man. So far his boss hadn't enquired too heavily about his progress, but he knew it couldn't be delayed for much longer.

Every morning Billy checked the top ten unsigned Internet acts. So far it had yielded him exactly nothing. Billy was undeterred. One afternoon after Easter he sat down at his desk to check the top ten and something miraculous happened. There at number eight in the chart was a band that looked exactly like the Desert Kings, only younger. He read the name back to himself "The RockAteers". He clicked the thumbnail and hoped to God they didn't sound awful. Once on their page he moved the cursor over to the music player box.

"They look the part but can they walk the walk?" he mumbled at his Mac. He clicked the first song "Bet On You" and sat back. By the time the first chorus kicked in, he was grinning. By the time the third chorus hit he had all his colleagues gathered around the desk to listen.

Egg – 11th May

Just got home from our first-ever proper gig in a venue. It was so crazy I thought I better document it properly, so here goes. Burt had been handing out RockATeers fliers all week and was expecting every teenage girl in the land to turn up. Bex was going to be there too. Since she started paying me more attention, Burt has been acting like an arse towards me. Bex said we would go shopping again before the gig, but then she said she couldn't because she had to work an extra shift at her dad's cab firm. She is the controller, which means she speaks to all the drivers. Sounds like a pretty important job.

I'd worn the clothes I got with Bex to death, so Burt said he would lend me something. It was the first time I'd ever been inside Burt's walk-in wardrobe. It was the size of my bedroom. I spent a long time staring at his clothes. I really had no idea what I should wear, so I just went with what he suggested, it was cool. His sister wasn't there this time. I think it's kind of odd there's only him in that huge house. My parents annoy me sometimes but I'm not sure I would want to live on my own.

Our social-media pages had been going mental the past couple of weeks with hundreds of likes a day and the play counter on the YouTube lyric videos has been going crazy. Each song has over 10,000 plays now. Burt says he's been posting links all the time but Tea reckons he's bullshitting. It's interesting because out of the three songs up, "Love and War" is in third place with 8,178 plays, "Satellites" is in 2nd place with 10,984 plays and "Bet On You" has 11,400 plays. Does that mean "Bet On You" is the best song, because I like "Satellites" better.

Clipper's dad has a van, and he took our gear to the venue. I hadn't met him before. He and Clipper are close. They were joking around a lot. Clipper's dad dropped us off outside with our gear. Burt had insisted that no parents were allowed to come to the gig. We had a long band argument about it as my dad really wanted to, as did Clipper's mum and dad. As usual Burt got his own way. Tea didn't say if his mum and dad wanted to come. I'm not sure he has parents. He never seems to have any limits on how late he can stay out, come to think of it. I don't even know where he lives.

Once we'd got everything inside the venue this cool-looking promoter bloke told us that we would be doing our sound check next and that we would be "sharing back line" and that the "foldback was really good" and that he'd hired some "wicked

monitors". The rest of the band looked confused
so I explained the lingo. Burt pointed out that
we needn't have bothered bringing our amps and
drum kit because all backline had been provided.
Tea pointed out that Burt should have told us that
before we roped Clipper's dad in to giving us a
lift. Sound check went quite smoothly. The sound
engineer was a little on the impatient and rude
side, but I couldn't fault the sound he was getting.

We had to wait for ages before doors opened at
7.30pm, so we hung around outside talking and
messing around. I kept looking out for Bex but
she didn't come early. Around 8.30 pm people
started arriving. That's when Burt went to work,
flitting from one group of people to the next as
if his nerves were made of wrought iron. My own
nerves were jangling, so the way he was acting
made me feel jealous. His good looks annoy me
too. I have developed a theory that Burt is so
good looking that he is almost anti-good looking,
as if he is so good looking that it's been
reversed and he is actually hideously repulsive.
I may be the only person that thinks that. I hope
Bex also thinks that.

Clip seemed better this time. Only three trips to
the toilet.

The venue held 500 and was about half full by the
time Microscope, the first band, went on stage.
They were a four piece but that's the only thing
they had in common with us. They wore spandex
and had big curly hair. Tea thought they were in
their mid-twenties, and I suppose it might have
been OK – if it was 1985. The singer was very
small. Clipper dubbed him Little Lycra Napoleon
which made Tea and me laugh loads. Before they'd

even played a note Little Lycra Napoleon was
stalking about the stage shouting at the crowd,
"Let me see your hands" and demanding they "clap"

When Microscope's first, terrible song started,
the singer started screaming at the crowd "Sing
it with me," and "We have been sent from Valhalla
to rock you!", leaning into the audience and
cupping his hand to his ear. The lack of reaction
made him mad.

"Do you want to rock?" he asked pointing his
microphone at them. Only one man shouted yes and
he looked like their mate; he was dressed the
same and was diving around like a demented flea.
The crowd just carried on talking.

"Do you want tooooooooo RRRRRRRRRRRAWK you
snivelling snot monkeys?"

Everyone went quiet then. Little Lycra Napoleon
had got their attention and pulled a theatrically
arrogant rock shape. Then the band crashed into
another song.

It was difficult to tell if it was an original
song. Little Lycra jumped about like a maniac,
yelling more than singing. His bandana-clad rock
hair obscured his face so that all you could
see was his bulbous nose. After only two songs
Microscope were dripping in sweat. I can't begin
to describe the music, so I won't try. "Not good"
covers it, and when the third song sounded even
worse I went outside to escape.

When I came back in five minutes later the stage
was empty. Clipper told me they'd been pulled off

because people had started to leave and beer cans were being hurled at Little Lycra.

"Why are Microscope called Microscope?" Tea asked me and Clipper. We both shook our heads, and he said: "Because you need one to see the lead singer?"

It was a stupid joke, but it made Clipper and I piss ourselves again. Then Burt came over looking smug and told us that the cool-looking promoter said Microscope had only brought one person when they had promised to bring fifty, so that was another reason why they got the chop early. Burt said we'd managed 166 people through the doors and the promoter was really happy with us. This only added to my unwavering fear.

The next offering were a band called Free Booze who had identical mop tops and baggy clothes, like the promoter. They played a few Desert Kings covers and to be honest, although pretty terrible, they were ten times better than Microscope. Then they'd finished and it was our turn.

My hands shook and my palms sweated as I set up my equipment. I was desperately trying not to look out at the hundreds of faces peering up at us from the dance floor. Once I'd finished arranging my guitar pedals, I studied the other boys. They all looked overwhelmed. Burt was struggling with his equipment. He scowled and gestured for me to go over. I sorted him out, returned to my spot and held my breath, I looked at Clipper and nodded. Clipper clicked his sticks four times and we were live.

Our set opener was "Love and War". We played
a few bum notes but got through it. When we
reached the end of the song I heard rapturous
applause. My spirits lifted and the nerves
started to go. By the second and third song we
were gathering momentum. The crowd seemed to
love it and despite the odd mistake from the
other lads we were playing well. Burt's voice
was clear and strong. Clipper's beat placement
was mostly solid. He has a habit of speeding up,
but it was bearable. At the end of the third
song even I was beginning to relax. By the time
Burt mumbled an introduction to one of our
rockier numbers, we were in the zone.

We reached halfway through the song and I
finally managed to look up at the audience. They
were pogoing. I couldn't believe it! I looked
over and saw that both Burt and Tea were head-
banging violently, flinging their long hair at one
another. I desperately wanted to join them in
this free expression, but I just couldn't find the
will. It was fascinating, considering their usual
interaction. I tried to remember what it reminded
me of. Suddenly I knew. They looked like the
70's rockers Status Quo when they did that whole
guitar dance thing.

Suddenly the wonderfulness all came crashing
down. In a particularly exaggerated head
banging flourish, Burt got his hair caught
in Tea's strings. What happened next was the
most incredible thing I have ever seen. As
Burt wheeled around frantically trying to free
himself, Tea, who could plainly see his band mate
was stuck, continued to pluck his bass strings,
hair and all.

I'm all for "the show must go on", but I did
think Tea should have stopped playing. He could
obviously see that Burt was caught up. I stopped
and then Clipper did too. We, along with the
500 spectators, stared at the carnage. It was
odd being able to hear a pin drop in a room with
so many people. I think it was why when Burt
shouted, "Get off me, you arse clown!" it seemed
so inappropriate.

Tea stopped strumming and tried to push Burt
away by his shoulders, yanking at his hair even
more. He screamed and started lashing out. When
a fist landed in Tea's face the crowd gasped in
shock. Tea looked steaming mad and started using
his bass as a battering ram, pushing it hard
into Burt's head. Then Burt kind of folded over
backwards and dragged Tea down with him. They
ended up in a heap on the floor, all hair and
flailing limbs.

That's when the laughter began, and when I say
laughter I mean total hysterics. Burt and Tea
wrestled and after what seemed like hours, but
must have been only a few seconds, Tea managed to
undo his guitar strap, freeing Burt to untangle
his hair. Like a pair of circus clowns they
stood up and stared out at the braying crowd
with a mixture of indignant rage and absolute
heartbreak.

The laughter died down and a hush fell over the
audience. Tea and Burt glowered at each other.
Then the crowd went mental, whooping, clapping
and whistling. Some people had held their mobile
phones up to record the mayhem.

Suddenly Burt's expression changed, from sullen, furious embarrassment, to all out basking joy. He threw his arms in the air, triumphantly stepping to the edge of the stage, smiling his charming smile. He cupped his hand to his ear, just like Little Lycra Napoleon, gesturing to his adoring fans that he wanted more. The crowd cheered louder. What balls, what bravado, what an absolute mad man he was! He walked over to an infuriated Tea and lifted his arm in a kind of faux boxing match climax. The crowd loved it! Burt picked his guitar from the stage floor, slung it about his neck, motioned to us and started strumming the chords to "Satellites". To my utter bewilderment we were going to carry on. Never did one man follow the command of Freddie Mercury, "the show must go on" with such fidelity. Burt was the craziest kid on the planet. It was official.

We brought 211 people to the gig in the end. The entry charge was five pounds and we got paid fifty-five pounds by the promoter. I told Burt that it was a pretty rough deal as it meant we were basically getting around 2.5% of the profits (and that was just from the people we brought in. If the full gate receipt was included then we were on something like 1%). He asked me which of those people I'd invited. When I said none, he told me to shut up. His logic made no sense to me but I did shut up.

If there is one thing that my life has a consistent habit of doing it's chopping me down just as I start feeling good about myself. I don't want to linger on the humiliating incident too long, it's too painful, but I promised myself I would document the entire night.

After the gig I stupidly went back to Burt's
house. I was in a really great mood, and Bex and
I were chatting loads. Later on I was standing
in the kitchen, facing everyone as they sat and
smoked and drank and talked around the big round
table. I was just in the middle of laughing at
a joke Tea was telling when I felt hands on my
trousers. Before I could stop it happening both
my jeans and pants were round my ankles and
everyone was in hysterics. I turned and saw Burt
and George behind me pissing themselves. I pulled
up my trousers and fled the house. I had just
about escaped the gravel courtyard when I heard
Bex calling me back. I couldn't even turn around.
I couldn't face her. I just ran.

Every time I seem to make headway Burt and George
ruin it all. They embarrassed me in front of
everyone, but most of all they humiliated me in
front of Bex. I have realised that as hard as I
try I will never be accepted. Even if this band
gets somewhere I will get my pants pulled down,
one way or another. Better to leave now before
something even worse happens to me.

From: The RockAteers [:therockateers@gmail.com]
To: Justin Clipper <Justin.clipper@gmail.com>,
Burt LBC <burtlbc@hotmail.com, Michael Twining
<teabag22@gmail.com>
Date: 12 May – 9.08am

Subject: I'm Out

Dear Lads,

I thought I'd do this over email because I really can't
deal with seeing anyone right now. Last night was the
final straw. When Burt and George shaved my eyebrows
off I decided I would carry on for the sake of our musical
unit. We have come so far and we proved that last night
I thought. But I can't handle the harassment anymore.
It's constant and cruel. So, I have decided to resign my
position in the band and concentrate on my exams. I wish
you all well. Even you, Burt.

Egg

From: Burt LBC <burtlbc@hotmail.com
To: Justin Clipper <Justin.clipper@gmail.com>, The
RockAteers [:therockateers@gmail.com], Michael
Twining <teabag22@gmail.com>
Date: 12 May – 1.32pm

Subject: RE I'm Out

Egg, you big ginger baby. So what if a few people saw your
little pink willy? #getoverit.

I will see you in rehearsals tomorrow. That's final.

From: Justin Clipper <Justin.clipper@gmail.com>
To: Burt LBC <burtlbc@hotmail.com, The RockAteers
[:therockateers@gmail.com], Michael Twining
<teabag22@gmail.com>
Date: 12 May – 1.39pm

Subject: RE RE I'm Out

Dear Egg,

Please don't leave. We have only just started getting really amazing and I love it. I think Burt and George were bang out of order pulling your pants down but it's not the end of the world and I really don't agree with Burt. I thought your dick was really big. In fact I was surprised at how big it was.

Please don't leave.

Big love Clip

From: Michael Twining <teabag22@gmail.com>
To: Burt LBC <burtlbc@hotmail.com, Justin Clipper
<Justin.clipper@gmail.com>, The RockAteers
[:therockateers@gmail.com],
Date: 12 May – 2.08pm

Subject: RE RE RE I'm Out

Clipper. That is possibly the gayest thing I've ever read. BUT, Egg, Clip is right, you have nothing to worry about in that department and you really shouldn't leave the band because of our tool bag of a singer. Burk, why can't you just say sorry instead of being such a stink hammer?

Tea

From: Burt LBC <<u>burtlbc@hotmail.com</u>
To: Justin Clipper <Justin.clipper@<u>gmail.com</u>>, The
RockAteers [:<u>therockateers@gmail.com</u>], Michael
Twining <<u>teabag22@gmail.com</u>>
Date: 12 May – 5.47pm

Subject: RE RE RE RE I'm Out

Clipper – I'm seriously worried about your sexuality.

Tea – Piss off and die. You think you're better than everyone else and you're not. You're just a whack bass player with a dodgy dress sense and a lightly caffeinated name.

Egg – I will see you down at rehearsal tomorrow. We will forget all about it. Yeah?

Clipper – 13th May

I have a proper big problem with emails that fly around between us in the band. I don't know why Burt sends such lairy ones all the time. He's either having a pop at one of us or they're unreadable. Like the one he sent about Hazel. She is totally our super fan. I think that's a good thing, but Burt reckons she's a stalker and calls her Crazel. I am pretty sure he already jumped her bones. Serves him right for being so good-looking! Anyway it doesn't matter now coz Egg sent us an email saying he's out of the band because he can't be in a band with Burt and he's sick of being bullied. He also wants to concentrate on revising for his exams. Why did Burt have to get mashed and pull Egg's trousers down? Now we don't got a guitarist or songwriter.

No one mentioned the George incident from the
last gig - thank God. I was dreading going into
school and being called stuff. Luckily no one has.

I still haven't told Dad I'm not gonna take the
place at Charlton Youth! I've still not played FIFA.

Wilson sat expressionless as he listened to The RockAteers.
"It's good!" he announced after a few bars. "And they look good
too. Well … three of them do!" He squinted at the photo on his
computer screen. "They're young. Sixteen, seventeen?"

"Younger I think," Billy Visconti said.

"They need work."

"Take a look at this, boss." Billy said, clicking on a new tab
and typing in the words Hair Guitar. The YouTube link came up
instantly. Billy clicked and sat back.

Billy watched as Cloom leaned further and further forward as
the two-minute clip played out. Act one – The big event. Act two
– The recognition. Act 3 – The musical climax. It had everything.
Despite the video being grainy and the sound being bad when the
band started to play, Billy knew they were gold. They looked and
lived the part. He had found his boss genuine rock'n'rollers! As
far as Billy was concerned it was mission accomplished.

"It's a sensation, Sir. They've had two million hits in less than
twenty-four hours. The sound is bang on and I'm positive the
Americans are gonna love it."

Cloom turned to Billy and nodded. "They need work!" he repeated.

"They do need a lot of work, but the formula is there, boss. This lot can shift units and I think "Bet On You" is a global hit. Billboard calibre. In fact, I'm sure of it!"

Cloom leant back in his chair and studied the picture of the band again. "Go and take a look at them," he said, with a nod. "Let's throw a bit of development money at them."

Billy frowned. "Boss, I have a good feeling about this lot. I think we need to sign them up sharpish. They're getting Internet hits like you wouldn't believe. The lead singer is unfeasibly good looking. They write amazing pop songs and they're volatile, which you and I know is a great PR angle. It won't be long before someone else gets a whiff and they're gone!"

"They'll have to change that God-awful name!"

"Granted it's bad, but I think that the band look cool enough for us to get away with it. I think we might be missing a trick. We spend a ton of money generating that kind of DIY profile. There is nothing like a real grass-roots buzz to kick off a campaign. I'd normally suggest we change the name after we sign them but in this case I really think the organic route is the right approach."

Billy didn't like the way Wilson was looking at him. "I'm not saying that our existing acts couldn't create a grass-roots groundswell," he spluttered. "It's just easier to synthetically accelerate that groundswell with money. People love to feel like they have discovered something for themselves."

"Are you teaching me to suck eggs, Visconti? The public don't go for a thing unless it's great. Remember that! Even if you believe that we decide what people are going to like, don't talk about it. A magician doesn't reveal his tricks." Cloom nodded towards the door.

"For some reason," he continued, "Joe Public think four skinny kids in tight jeans with long hair are in some way cooler than four neat boys in suits sitting on stools. Personally I think coolness should be judged on singing ability and nine times out of ten the boys sitting on stools win hands down!"

Billy took a step towards the door. "So can I make an offer?"

"Bring them to me," Cloom replied.

Burt – 18th May

Egg hasn't returned any of my phone calls, texts or emails. It's been a week. I was thinking of sending a letter but I'm actually not sure how to do that. It wasn't anything to do with me. What is he playing at? I've left him about a million messages, the tit. Billy Visconti from Big Tone records has emailed our RockAteers address twice and asked if he can come to a rehearsal ASAP. This is the big time. What's up with him?

Bex has taken his side and is acting like she hates me. It was bad enough when she didn't fancy me but now I've actually lost ground. I was just about to put my plan of acting like Egg into action as well! I don't know how I'll cope if Bex carries on ignoring me.

In other apocalyptic news the idiot known as Crazel has now got hold of my mobile number and

she keeps calling me and leaving mental messages.
When I get mashed I sometimes feel tempted to
get her round but then after about five minutes
I realise that's pure madness. What about the
standing outside my house after we got jiggy?
I'm worried she might tell Bex that we had sex.
I think it's exactly the kind of thing she might
do. That really would ruin things for me.

So now Big Tone wants to see us and everything's
pretty crazy. So I'm taking control of the
situation. Ego Egg wrote the lyrics "All's fair
in love and war". He better believe it coz I'm
going off the reservation on this one. (Mills, if
you're reading this let me translate – I'm doing
things my way from now on and I start tomorrow,
at 2pm to be exact.)

✪

SONG 7 APOLOGIES

Burt arrived at Big Tone Records alone. He had decided that under no circumstances could the band lose out on this opportunity, and he was damned if someone was going to ruin his dream of being a rock star by coming along to the meeting and acting like a bastard. Sir Wilson Cloom was the most important person in music. If Egg didn't own a TV and wasn't aware of that fact it was his problem. Burt wasn't going to let Egg's pig-headedness drag the band down with him.

Wilson Cloom made people's dreams happen and Billy Visconti was his heir apparent; at least that's what Visconti had intimated to Burt on the phone. When Billy had suggested that the band come in for a meeting at the label, Burt had jumped at the chance. So what if the rest of the band wouldn't be there? He was the talent.

When Burt stepped into the foyer of Big Tone Records he couldn't help feeling overwhelmed by its grandeur and style. The huge space, which housed around ten other subsidiary imprint labels, immediately impressed him. The space was cool and ultra modern, with a long row of desks along the far wall with seven or eight smartly dressed receptionists manning each station. On the high ceiling an impressive ring of flat screen televisions flashed images of acts signed to Big Tone and the other labels. Burt informed one of the receptionists that he was there to see Sir Wilson Cloom. He was handed a plastic visitor's pass and told to wait on one of the luxurious sofas dotted around the foyer.

Once seated, Burt marvelled at just how many cool-looking people were milling around and wondered how many of them knew or worked with the famous. A second later he wasn't thinking about people who *knew* famous people any more. He was in the presence of one. There, only a few feet from him, was Lily Vendetta. She had nearly won Sir Wilson Cloom's *X-Finder* that year and now she had a recording deal and was always in *Heat*. Burt couldn't believe it when she looked him up and down. Did she just check him out?! Suddenly he didn't care because the most beautiful and sophisticated girl Burt had ever set eyes on walked straight up to him. For a moment he thought it was Cheryl Cole.

"Wilson and Billy will see you now, Mr Skill. Please come with me," she said in what Burt thought sounded like Queen's English.

Burt rocketed from the sofa. As he followed, he paid close attention to the outline of her behind in the short pencil skirt and repeated the new name he had given himself just hours before. James Burt Windsor just didn't cut it. If Bono and Sting could do it then why couldn't Jack Skill? He said the name over in his head a few more times. Yes, it was brilliant. Clipper and Tea had been unsure about the name change, of course, but as they didn't have a stylish bone between them he had ignored their input.

As they went toward the lifts he racked his brain for something witty or cool to say. It was hard to concentrate in the company of such perfect, tanned legs. Once inside the elevator, she pressed the button for the twentieth floor, turned and gave him a warm smile.

"Do you come here often?" Burt blurted.

The beauty smiled. "Well, let's see. I work here, so yes, I suppose I do."

Burt fell silent. The lift doors dinged and she led him through a plush open-plan administrative area until they reached a large glass-fronted office. Inside, using the telephone at his desk, was a man he recognised. Though he had known he would meet him for most of the day, nothing could have prepared Burt for the shock of seeing the most famous man in UK pop. The music mogul looked exactly as he did on TV, only shorter. He wore a cream sweater, smart black suit trousers and cowboy boots. His face looked stretched and his hair was a strange shade of brown. Burt wondered if it was true what the papers said – that he used botox and wore a wig. Suddenly he felt completely out of his depth.

"Sit," said the girl, pointing to a waiting area. "Wilson won't be long. Would you like a tea, or coffee?"

Unable to speak, Burt shook his head. He slumped into the waiting chair and watched as she took her seat at a nearby desk. After an agonizing ten-minute wait he was suddenly confronted by a man dressed in smart Converse pumps, a baseball jacket and Dolce & Gabbana jeans.

"You must be Jack Skill," he said, holding out a hand with a confident smile. "I'm Billy Visconti."

Oh God. His new name. Did it sound cool? He could only grin in response as he shook the man's hand.

"Nice to put a face to a name. I've been so psyched to meet you." Visconti waited for a response, but none came.

"Come on," he continued jovially. "Let's go in and I'll introduce you to the great man himself."

Burt followed Billy into the corner office and looked around nervously. The sprawl of London Town was right there through the windows, like a postcard. The view was breathtaking; from the Shard to the Gherkin and the City then down the Thames past the Eye. It was magic.

"Dear boy, welcome to my office in the sky!" announced the familiar voice from behind the desk. "*Charlie and the Great Glass Elevator* was my favourite story growing up. If you dream something hard enough, it will come true!" He rose from his chair, walked around the table and extended a hand in greeting. "I'm Wilson. You must be Jack Skill."

Burt nodded awkwardly, once again regretting the name change.

"Where's the band?" Wilson asked, re-occupying his plush leather chair. Burt had already noted that his seat was much higher up than those he and Billy were sitting in. Burt had heard about this trick before somewhere. It was all about power.

"Er … they couldn't make it."

Wilson glanced at Billy. Billy acknowledged the pass and turned to Burt.

"So, can you tell us a little bit about the band?" he asked.

"Like what?"

"Like … how old you all are, who writes the songs, what your ambitions are, who you think your music is aimed at?"

"Well … we're all sixteen, except the guitarist who is fifteen," Burt said, counting the answers off on his fingers. "And … we

113

all go to the same school, we all love The Desert Kings and … I suppose my songs are aimed at everybody!" Burt shuffled in his chair with four fingers held aloft. "Was that it?"

"Ambitions?" Billy prompted helpfully.

"To be the biggest rock band on the planet!"

"Ha, if I had a penny for every time I had heard that one I'd be an even richer man than I am already." Wilson leant forward slightly. "Are you aware of just how much hard work goes into making that a reality?"

"I think so," Burt said blankly. Wilson stared back at the teenager.

"I mean, I'm willing to find out," Burt went on. "If you give me a chance, I mean. You know, if you give *us* a chance then we will prove how hard we can work."

The older men looked at one another and smiled.

"You have an amazing following on Twitter and Facebook, that YouTube vid 'Hair Guitar' is genius," Billy said. "I don't think I've seen a buzz like that since Bieber. How did all that come about?"

"Dunno really. We did a couple of gigs and made a demo and then everyone just loved it."

"It's the songs, Jack!" Wilson pointed at him. "You have great songs. You're the singer right? Do you compose the tunes as well?"

"Yes, I'm the singer. Er … yes, I also write the songs too," Burt said touching his nose.

"And would you be prepared to make sacrifices, if it was for the good of the music?" Wilson asked.

"Of course I would. I just want to be out there touring, making the music, living the dream, you know?"

"I do know!" replied Wilson, a smile forming on his lips. "You want me to make you a star?"

Burt's eyes lit up and he nodded frantically.

Tea – 25th May

We work our balls off and then just when we start to get somewhere Jack or Burt or whatever he has decided to call himself this week pulls our songwriter's pants down in front of everyone! The conniving little tool bag wanted me to go round Egg's house to apologise for him and explain that Wilson Cloom is interested in signing the band, so could he please come back to rehearsals? Why are we going with the first person that flutters their eyelashes at us anyway? We have only been a band for nine months. Wilson Cloom is the guy that signed all the biggest pop bands in the country. We're a rock band that does the occasional ballad, not a boy band that does the occasional reality show. Not that it matters, because Jack Burk tit balls persuaded me to go and see Egg tonight didn't he? At the beginning of the conversation I had absolutely no intention of doing what he asked, but he wears you down with constant nagging until you can't think straight anymore. Thing is, I just really want this band to work. School and exams don't stimulate me and I can't live the rest of my life on the estate I was born on. It's simply not an option.

Clipper - 25th May

Burt phoned and told me that none other than Sir Wilson Cloom is interested in signing the band! I nearly soiled myself. How wicked is that!!? Burt then started going on about how important it was to get Egg back in the band. So eventually I rung Egg's parents' house, coz his mum won't let Egg have a mobile, which I think is well mean. His mum told me he hadn't been to school because he has taken time off to study for the exams and she said I wasn't allowed to speak to him. Thing is I know that's a lie and he hasn't come to school coz he got his pants pulled down. So me and Tea went round there. His mum was pretty scary and off with us when she answered the door, but I told her we didn't have anything to do with the shaving of his eyebrows or the pulling his trousers down incidents and that I had actually beaten the kid up that did both things to him. She just stared at me blankly for ages as if she was a bit mental, but then she let us in. I see now where Egg gets his uncontrollable ginger barnet from.

As soon as we saw Egg I knew he would come back. He was so pleased to see us. Tea played a blinder. "Burk has changed his name to Jack Skill and is talking to Wilson Cloom on his own, do you really want that massive weapon to ruin our band?" That really did the trick coz Egg said he would come back to rehearsals.

I wanted to tell Egg that I dreaded going into school every day and seeing George ever since the whole him accusing me of being gay thing happened, but I couldn't tell him because I was still too embarrassed. I just can't seem to get the whole thing out of my head, and even though no one has said anything yet, it feels like it's

hanging over my head like a noose. It's true what
they say about words hurting more than blows.

I still haven't told my dad I chose music over
football.

"Are you actually mental?" Bex asked as they sat on High
Bench. Burt had named it High Bench because it overlooked all
of London and stood on the topmost point in Greenwich Park. If
it wasn't freezing or raining, it was where Burt conducted all his
important meetings. It was where he split up with girls and where
he came to contemplate.

It was a fiercely hot spring day and Burt was struggling to
recover his composure since Bex had turned up in cut-off denim
shorts so tiny the inside pockets were visible. Her flawless olive
skin was glistening in the sun. Burt found it impossible to concentrate, but it was crucial he appeared sensitive.

"I'm not mental. It will work, and you only have to do it for a
week or so."

"Can I be totally honest?" Bex asked, standing up. Burt
gawped at her long, tanned legs. She folded her arms.

"Please do," Burt replied, faking a posh accent. "But before
you do can I just say that I am extremely sensitive to your needs.
I'd say six times more sensitive than Egg is."

Bex frowned and shook her head. "OK … let's see … where
do I start: you're the best-looking boy in school, you're rich, you

have a gang of beautiful friends hanging off your every word, and now you're in a rock band that, I think, is going places. Problem is, you're not a very nice person!"

Burt looked confused for a moment. "So you think I'm the best-looking kid in school? Better-looking than Tea?"

Bex sighed. She sat back down and gazed across the London skyline.

"Burt, I don't fancy you, and I think this plan of yours is just some kind of lame attempt to sabotage mine and Egg's friendship. I think you're proper jealous of Egg's genius. For all those reasons, I'm out."

Burt stared at her. "OK, OK," he said eventually, "I don't think you understand what I was trying to say! I don't want you to sleep with him or anything. You shouldn't… I mean, you don't even have to kiss him. I just want you to make him feel like he is part of the gang."

"You really are the stupidest boy I've ever met! I know exactly what you're trying to say. You're manipulating a situation and using people as pawns in your quest for fame!" She paused. "I'll put it another way. I … am … *not … doing … it*."

Burt looked at Bex in startled confusion. "No, no, Bex, listen. You really don't understand. I'm trying to get you to go out with Egg for a week so that he will stay in the band! How's that manipulating anyone? How's that using people as pawns? Don't you see how hard I've worked on my sensitive side?"

Bex kissed her teeth. "I'm off," she said. She got up and started down the hill towards Greenwich Village.

"By the way," Burt shouted after her, looking utterly perplexed,

"I'm not jealous of him… So get your facts straight. How could I be jealous of that tosser?"

Bex carried on down the hill without looking back.

Burt stayed in his favourite spot, reluctant to leave until he had figured out what had just happened. Where had the plan gone wrong? After thinking about it harder than he'd ever thought about anything in his entire life, he concluded that deep down Bex did indeed fancy him, and that this was the real reason why she wouldn't go out with Egg. She couldn't face being with anyone else.

The remark about him not being a very nice person kept coming back to him. He was just concluding that this was down to her inability to come to terms with her feelings for him, when his thoughts were interrupted by a familiar voice from behind.

"Burt! Fancy seeing you here!"

Burt turned to see Hazel beaming down at him.

"Cr— Hazel!" he grinned awkwardly. "What you doing here?"

"It's OK, you can call me Crazel. I know that's my nickname. I'm not stupid." She plonked herself down on the bench, closer to Burt than he felt comfortable with. "You can call me anything you like, Burt. You know that."

As she leant in for a kiss, Burt shot backwards as far as the bench would allow and stared back at her, panic stricken.

"My *name* is Jack!"

Hazel let out a long groan, raising her arms and pushing out her large chest in a long, seductive yawn. Burt studied her; she reminded him of a teenage Drew Barrymore. Her button nose wrinkled and large hazel eyes widened as he took her in. She wore cherry-red lipstick and her brilliant white teeth dazzled every time she smiled. He liked her style. She was quirky. If only she wasn't bonkers.

"Sorry, I forgot," she said, flicking her shoulder-length bleached hair. "Only I've been up all night."

"Yeah? Doing what?"

"Facebook. Twitter and stuff," she murmured, looking away towards the Observatory. "Posting stuff about the band," she added after a pause, stifling another yawn.

"Band? What band?"

She smiled at him. "Your band, stupid. I suppose you could say that I've taken on the unofficial role of the online RockAteers promoter. Why do you think you have so many fans? I've been at it for months now. I just started a RockAteers Instagram as well, like, with gig pics and other cool stuff."

"Really?" Burt asked, relaxing a little, the compliments calming him.

She shuffled toward him an inch. "I mean, it's easy to get fans, of course. How could anyone resist how absolutely gorgeous you all are and the amazing songs you write? I know all the words to all the songs, you know!"

"You do? And what … you actually talk to people about the band … online?"

"*Duh*, Of course I do. For the past six months I've been on my laptop every night talking to all your fans. People love you. Don't you get it?"

Burt frowned. "Who do they think is the best-looking then?"

"You, silly! I mean people think Tea is pretty fit as well of course – you know, that rough and ready, bad boy look – but I'd say you are definitely out in front." She paused and shifted a further inch. "Personally I think you're the best-looking by a mile."

"I'm a bad boy as well, though," Burt said with a scowl.

"Oh no, no," she said, moving to calm him. "You *are* a bad boy, and you're rough and ready. You're the best, Burtie … I mean … Jack!"

"I guess so." Burt eyed her carefully. She was nearly fit but the clothes were bad. She did have all the right bits and in all the right places. He shook his head as if to rid himself of thoughts of her physicality. Once was enough. Never get back into a cold bath was his motto.

"Do you want to go for a coffee, and I'll fill you in on all the goings-on in cyber world?"

Burt stood up like a jack-in-the-box. "No, no…", he spluttered, his mind racing as he tried to come up with an excuse. "I've got to go over there now!"

He pointed down the hill toward Greenwich Village before setting off at a pace.

"OK, see you soon, Burtie," he heard Hazel call after him. "Don't be a stranger!"

Egg – 30th May
Burt has left me a million messages. He never actually apologised in any of them. He tried to

get me excited about this Wilson Cloom but he never actually said sorry. His next cunning move was to send Tea and Clipper round. It worked. I agreed that I would go back, mainly because I can't be bothered to talk about it anymore.

Mum is still furious even though my eyebrows have totally grown back. She said I wasn't allowed to go back to the band. We had another big family meeting and my dad stuck up for me. She used the old classic of me being only fifteen but I said that I was sixteen in a couple of months and that if she didn't let me go back to the band I would move out as soon as it was legal. Finally she gave in, although I did have to re-promise to get good marks in my exams, which start next week.

Bex came round yesterday. Luckily my mum was at work when she arrived. Dad sent her straight up to my room. Bex in my messed-up bedroom was not cool. I suppose I never believed she would ever be within two miles of my bedroom let alone inside it. I got all flustered and started scooping boxer shorts off the floor. I couldn't stop thinking about her having seen my penis.

Because it was baking hot outside she was wearing tight red shorts and a vest top. Her cleavage was amazing. And on top of me not being able to look at her, my bedroom floor is covered in pants.

Straight off she hit me with the news that Burt had asked her if she would go out with me as a ploy to get me to rejoin the band!

I was stunned. Eventually I said that I'd already

agreed to go back to the band and didn't really understand what was going on.

Why was she here in my bedroom wearing shorts? Looking really amazing! Why did she want me to know that Burt wanted her to be my charity girlfriend? I already know he's a complete tit. Why didn't she just not tell me?

So I said. "Why would you want to go out with an idiot like me for a week anyway? That would be mental!"

She rested her hand on my knee. On any other day I would have loved it, but I was really angry and I shrugged it off. "Why don't you run back to your pimp," is what I said. I have no idea what came over me.

So then she gets up and gives me a look that would stun a lion and just leaves. Why did I say that? Why? Burt manages to spoil everything. Even when he's not there.

I sat in my dungeon of a bedroom for about twenty-four hours and wrote a song about deep and painful loss. It's called "Deadbeat Poets" and the words just fell out of me. They don't seem to be that literal in meaning, but I think what I am trying to say is that I am a deadbeat and that I would do anything for a girl called Bex. What kind of poet kicks the best thing in his life out of his house?

I am happy with the lyrics but I'm not sure about making up a word. I've written a lot of songs but never made up a word before. The word I made up is juxtaprose. It's an amalgamation of the words juxtapose, meaning contrasting opposites and the word prose, meaning writing style in its simplest form. Basically it's a dig at pretentious poets thinking they can make up stupid words and put them in love songs.

Deadbeat Poets

Verse 2:
1st stanza
And all those deadbeat poets sat there
Writing juxtaprose
Can keep their half-cocked love streams
Coz pretention smells so old

Tea entered the school hall half expecting not to see Egg. But there he was, setting up his guitar amp in the usual methodical way he always did. He looked over to Burt's station and saw to his surprise that he too was setting up his gear, in his usual slapdash super-fast manner.

"Hello lads," Tea said, concealing his relief. Tea had changed his opinions on a lot of stuff over the past few months. He no longer felt angry towards Burt, he really loved being in the band

and had even got used to the rock'n'roll uniform he had to wear.

When Clipper walked in carrying his large bass-drum case, which always caused him to walk lopsided, Tea was suddenly overcome with a feeling he hadn't experienced before. He felt truly sentimental at the sight of all four of them in the room together again.

As he unfurled his leads and took his bass pedals from their box, Tea thought about Clipper and how much he liked him. He was one of the nicest people he had ever met. "Bollocks, I'm getting soppy," he said under his breath, as he took his Fender bass out of its case.

The RockAteers finished setting up in silence. Clipper clicked his sticks four times and the band crashed into their half-hour set. It was great to play together again and the nine songs ran seamlessly despite the break. Once they had gone through the songs, Burt put his hand up, calling the attention of the room. Tea continued to noodle.

"Jesus, Tea," said Burt. "Can't you shut up for more than five seconds?"

Tea stopped for a moment, smiled and carried on noodling.

"We need to have a conversation," Burt said loudly. The noodling stopped. Egg's shoulders dropped visibly.

"Why do we always get into long conversations about everything?" Tea protested. "Why can't we just play music?"

"Because," Burt said, more quietly, "because I have something important to tell you."

"OK, what is it?" Tea said, putting his bass on his lap.

"I went to see Sir Wilson Cloom this week and he wants us to do a showcase gig." Egg's shoulders dropped further still. Tea looked confused. Clipper jumped up from his stool.

"That's ace, ace, ace!" he shouted.

"Couldn't you have waited till we could all go together?" Egg asked, exhaling noisily.

"No I couldn't, you idiot. If we had waited for you we'd have missed out on a big opportunity. You weren't answering any of my calls, remember? I didn't want to ruin our chances, so I took one for the team. I don't think you realise just how difficult and stressful the meeting was. I really had to convince them that we are the best band around."

"You were sulking, Egg," Tea said.

"Give me a break. First he shaves my eyebrows off and then he pulls my pants down and doesn't even say sorry. Then he tries to get a girl to go out with me because he thought somehow it would make me want to rejoin the band."

"Don't be daft. I did say sorry. It was George anyway. And I don't know what you're talking about. What girl—?" Burt stared at Egg for a moment. "Bex," he murmured, under his breath.

"Bex is … lying!" he said unconvincingly.

"No. You're lying," Egg replied.

Clipper stood up and hit his snare hard three times. "Lads, lads, lads. What are we doing? Why are we bickering? What does it matter who did what when? Of course Burt—"

"And that's another thing. From now on, can everyone remember to call me Jack Skill? Please?"

"OK," conceded Clipper. "Of course *Jack* should have waited to go and see Wilson, but we need to get over it. Surely the music

126

is bigger than any one of us and all that stuff. I don't know anything about 'getting Bex to go out with Egg' but if you think about it, if it was true, and I'm not saying it is, then it just goes to show how desperate Burt is – I mean Jack is – to make this band work." He paused and gave Egg a pleading look. "Surely that counts for something, mate?"

Egg remained silent for a few moments before nodding curtly.

"True dat!" Tea said. "You tell 'em, Clip!"

The band agreed to talk less and play more and spent the rest of the rehearsal getting the music slick and tight for the Sir Wilson Cloom showcase.

SONG 8 PROMISES

"How's the RockAteers showcase shaping up?" Wilson asked.

"All set," Billy replied. "The Borderline has the right vibe and won't overwhelm them. It's a good little venue and I think the West End of London is the right location. All the heads of department are coming, the in-house radio people are on the list and I have the usual press agents primed and ready."

"And how are you going to create that Desert Kings vibe?"

Billy looked puzzled. "Er … well … the band are inviting their friends and fans, so the vibe should be created organically."

"Terrific. I want the band on the label, Billy, so let's make sure we seal the deal on the night, OK? We don't need to get things signed, that's unrealistic. Let's just make sure we turn on the charm and land the deal … make sure you get a firm handshake on the night and all that. Are we clear?"

Billy nodded soberly and left Wilson's office. As he paced through the musical corridors of power, he recalled his meeting with Wilson and Jack. Billy couldn't put his finger on it, but something wasn't quite right about Jack Skill. He knew beneath the initial whiff of nerves that the kid had charisma by the bucket-load, great looks and could certainly hold a note, but something still worried him; something about the kid's character, perhaps.

Was he deceitful? He had been around some of the slyest operators in the world so he certainly had the radar for it.

By the time he reached his desk he was totally convinced that something about the teenager just didn't fit. It was the little things that obsessed Billy, and it was why at only twenty-four he was one of the most powerful and wealthy junior operators in the business. Wilson wanted The RockAteers bad and Billy needed to deliver them. The total change of style was the worrying thing for Billy and was why he was so nervous around his boss. Big Tone Records signed pop. This was uncharted territory. If he didn't pull it off, it would mean serious consequences. There must be no mistakes. Finally, his gut feeling was too strong to ignore. He decided to go and meet the entire band before the showcase.

Egg – 26th June
I've tried to get in touch with Bex for over two weeks now but she is unresponsive. I've seen her hanging out after exams over the past few days but she ignores me. I have an inability to confront people anyway, especially if they're within a few feet of another person, so I decided to apologise using the most cowardly, faceless medium, the phone. And that meant using our crap, brown relic of a house phone (I need a mobile so bad. Kids in the third world are more digitally advanced than me). Of course, she didn't answer. I started off with messages like:

"Listen, I'm really sorry, Bex. Can we meet up? I was having a bad day. I didn't mean to ask you to leave."

After a couple of days, when she still hadn't got back to me, I started leaving messages like:

"Come on, Bex. I couldn't be sorrier. I was an idiot. I was worse than an idiot. I was the worst kind of idiot."

After seven days I just flat out started to beg. By the time two weeks of silence rolled round I was beside myself.

"Bex, I'm going crazy here. If you don't phone me soon I think I might have to jump off a bridge."

Not my proudest moment, but it did work (sort of) because just a few minutes later she phoned back. This is what she said before hanging up...

"Egg, please don't phone again. If you do then I am going to tell my father to come round to your house and actually kill you. It will be a lot easier than jumping off a bridge because you won't actually have to go to the trouble of leaving the house."

I wish she would send her dad round to kill me.

Tea – 27th June
I am actually excited. Yes, it's true. Tomorrow this bloke from Big Tone Records is going to take us for a posh dinner. So far Burt the Flirt (or Jack tit balls as I like to call him nowadays) has been keeping all the managerial stuff close

to his chest and I don't trust him. He keeps
saying that whilst we don't have a manager he is
the next best thing to one and that if we don't
believe him then how comes we have a showcase
with the most powerful man in pop. Egg pointed
out that we are a real live band and that we only
just started a year ago and why are we jumping
through hoops for this guy, but like I said, Burt
is the most persuasive man on the planet.

Burt and Egg have a really strained relationship
now. It worries me a bit. Anyway I think it's
going to be cool. The songs are sounding tight as
arseholes and we break up for the summer holidays
in a week.

Billy took The RockAteers to the most expensive restaurant in
Greenwich. Once the band was seated in the plush surroundings
of the piano bar, he kicked off with a tricky question.

"So how is your publishing going to be split? I understand
that Jack writes the songs? Jack, have you thought about giving a
percentage to the rest of the band?"

Billy felt the atmosphere change. Jack's head dropped into the
menu and the other band members stared at him in confusion.

"Right, that's my mistake. In our meeting with Wilson I
asked Jack who writes the songs. I also asked him a lot of other
questions all at the same time. He was obviously just confused.
Sorry. It's my fault."

The band looked unconvinced. Billy continued steadily. "Look,

guys, I'm not going to lie. I think you have all the ingredients …
songs, lyrics, image and youth. I think the sky's the limit. If you
perform at the showcase like you did in that rehearsal then I'm
sure we will be offering you a deal."

Billy watched three faces light up. Egg was unmoved, wary,
almost angry. Billy knew what he had to do.

"You write the songs don't you, Egg?" Billy asked softly.

Egg nodded cautiously.

"Well, I want to tell you something," Billy leant across the
table and took hold of Egg's shoulder. "The words and melodies
you weave are some of the most haunting I have ever heard. You
have the lyrical skill of Bob Dylan, the musicality of the Beatles
and the melody of Robbie Williams. He paused to gauge Egg's
reaction. "I hope none of those comparisons are offensive. I just
love your work, man."

Egg replied with a grimace and Billy knew he had a tough
one on his hands; the kind of creative that neither compro-
mised his art nor took compliments with enthusiasm. It worried
him. He hadn't worked with an artist he couldn't manipulate
through praise.

Clipper – 27th June
I really used to look up to Burt for ages but
now I am beginning to think he's just a massive
bastard. I've just come back from a well nice
restaurant Billy Visconti took us to. He is
really funny and dead fashionable and has a
Mohawk haircut. Everything was going great. Billy

loved our rehearsal at school and was tapping
his foot and nodding his head all the way through
the set. Then we go to the restaurant and Billy
says he thought Jack wrote all the songs. So Burt
has obviously lied to him because he looked well
guilty. After that revelation Billy gets down
to asking us loads of questions. Like where do
we see the band going? And what do we want from
a life on the road? He was really interested in
all our answers, even though Burt tried to answer
them all for us, as if we would mess it all up.
The cheek of Burt is mental considering what had
just happened. The dinner was well upper class.
I had a steak tatare, which is basically mashed
up steak meat with green bits in. When I got it
Tea told me I was a nob for ordering raw meat
but I actually really liked it. Egg was really
quiet all the way through the meal. Billy kept on
trying to bring him into the conversations but
Egg was having none of it.

Afterwards when me and Egg were walking home he
told me that he wasn't sure we should trust Billy
Visconti. I told him that I thought he was very
generous and that the meal must have cost a ton of
money so we shouldn't judge him so quickly. "That's
why you will always be a better man than me, Clip."
I didn't really understand what that meant but I
was glad to see him smile. I'm well drunk – four
pints of Peroni in two-and-a-half hours.

I lied to my dad yesterday and said I am all
prepared to start youth academy. It's getting
pretty stupid now.

"Jack isn't the songwriter, the ginger guitarist is," Billy told Wilson as the pair sat in the deluxe company canteen.

"Jack's the driving force though, as ambitious as they come. I am certain he would do anything to get this deal, boss. Incidentally Jack Skill seems to be his stage name. The rest of the band accidentally called him Burt all the way through our meal."

Wilson nodded. "What about the other two?"

"The bass player is kind of moody and I think the big drummer is gay."

"Gay?"

"As in he likes boys."

"Don't get smart with me, Visconti! So Jack, or whatever his name is, lied to us?"

Billy nodded solemnly. "Twice."

"Bands," Wilson said casually, finishing his pomegranate juice before getting up to leave. Billy followed Wilson back through the corridors towards his office. He listened in obedient silence to Wilson's walking monologue:

"You see, Visconti, this is exactly why I don't get involved with anyone who talks back or has an opinion. The Music Business has two very distinct words in it: Music, and Business. When the product or music is made then I take over! I do the business. I've been working on a formula to cut out the need for the artist all my life but I haven't come up with a solution." He shook his head, almost talking to himself. "They seem to be an inescapable necessity!"

Wilson stopped abruptly, turned and fixed Billy with a hard stare. "We aren't going to have any trouble from these guys, are we?"

Billy shook his head frantically.

"Terrific." Cloom's voice sank to a whisper. "Because if you screw this up, I will have your guts for garters."

Egg – 3rd July
I just got back from rehearsal and I'm feeling pretty mad. Burt going around telling people he writes the songs is bordering on corrupt. I looked up publishing on the Internet to see what the usual splits are between bands. My findings were inconclusive. Some bands split it equally, regardless of who writes the songs, and some bands split it 25% lyrics, 25% vocal melodies, 50% music and arrangements.

At rehearsals tonight I told the boys we should talk about publishing. I said that we should split the songs 52% me, and that they take the remaining 48%, 16% each. Clipper and Tea just nodded and said that it was cool but Burt went mental. I mean here is a guy that claimed to write all my songs and didn't even apologise, and now he is having a go at me because I'm giving him a cut of the publishing, even though he didn't write any of the bloody songs! He said I was a selfish wanker and that I was nothing without him. If it wasn't for the fact that the songs are sounding so good I would have just left the band right there and then. Even though I'm seething with Burt right now I'm not an idiot. I know he's really good-looking and that I couldn't front a band, but I did write the bloody songs – doesn't that count for something? Shouldn't I get what's fair? I think I deserve it.

Billy was right when we went out for dinner with him. Combine looks and youth with great songs and you have a sure-fire hit. I can see that, but I am only fifteen. Why can't it just be about the music until I am older and can't afford to eat? I can sell my soul to the devil then! Only a week before the big showcase and already I can't sleep. The worst thing is that Bex still hasn't phoned me back. That she will never speak to me again has started to sink in.

Burt – 3rd July
That thieving little turd. If he thinks that he is gonna drive around in a Lamborghini while I can only afford a Mini Cooper then he can think again (I realise I already have a Lambo). Everyone knows that the money is in the songwriting and the touring. There's no way he's getting more than me, the ginger git. Without me he is just another ugly face with a few half decent songs. I'm the one that's gonna have to put my neck on the line. I'm the one that will get chased by loads of paparazzi when we're famous. Why shouldn't I get the same cut of the dollars? Why didn't he come and discuss it with me separately? We could have offered the other two a smaller amount, like the split could go 40/40 for me and Smeg and 10/10 for Clip and Tea. No one cares about the rhythm section. Also everybody knows that bands last longer if they split things more equally. Anyway I think I made the fool see sense because he didn't say anything after I had a go at him.

Bex stood nervously on Egg's front porch, her finger hovering over the doorbell. She'd missed Egg over the past few weeks, but had sworn to herself that, after the unforgivable things he had said, he would receive four weeks' punishment. A month was a sufficient sentence, she felt. It had been hard to stick to, but she had achieved it. It had been especially difficult given the volume and type of the phone calls she had received from him. Bex knew exactly why Egg had been so upset and had said such horrible things to her, but she felt it was important to teach him a lesson, so that he would never do anything like that again.

Before she lost her nerve, Bex pushed hard on the doorbell. The door opened quickly.

"Bex! What are you doing here?"

Bex studied him. Egg's hair was longer, his glasses and spots had vanished.

"Wow! You look wicked." she declared. "How you doin'?"

She smiled, watching as the surprise spread across his face. She had forgotten how much she liked his out-of-proportion handsomeness. He looked interesting and wise. Sorting out his image had clearly done a huge amount for his confidence. Contact lenses instead of glasses and skin care had rendered him tolerable to the likes of someone like Burt, but she had agreed to help him for another reason. She wanted to relieve Egg's crippling lack of confidence. She wanted to help him for his sake. That Burt had paid for the transformation was ironic.

Suddenly Bex realised that she had been staring silently at Egg for longer than was usual and he was starting to look a little uncomfortable. Before she could speak she noticed something else that was fresh about Egg and it was the most striking difference of all. He seemed to be developing muscles on his skinny frame.

"You been working out, Egg?" she asked, pushing past him and into the house. "Hello, Mrs Poacher," she added brightly, spotting Egg's mum in the kitchen.

Egg followed her into the hall, narrowly avoiding his mum's glare.

"Er … yes. Burt thought it might be a good idea if we all looked a bit trimmer. He told us that the Desert Kings work out so maybe we should too."

"Did he? LOL! That boy really does have an obsession." Egg showed her into the front room and Bex plonked herself on the sofa.

"It's great to see you," he said, sitting down in the armchair opposite. "But … well, why exactly are you here? Don't get me wrong, I'm over the moon you're here but … well I mean… I thought you weren't talking to me?"

Suddenly Egg's mum was in the room, scowling. "What can I do for you?" she said, glaring down at Bex.

Egg looked distraught.

"I've come to speak to Egg," Bex replied.

"What about? He's left that silly band and isn't interested in fancy clothes or a girlfriend who humiliates him."

"Mum, she's not my girlfriend!" Egg said, blushing deeply. "And she didn't humiliate me."

Bex gathered herself. "I like your son, Mrs Poacher. I think he's talented, proper smart and great to hang about with. He's my mate, but if you have a problem with the way I look, then that's your thing, not mine. I came here to forgive him for saying some pretty hurtful things."

Carol frowned and turned her attention to Egg. "What did you do, Egg?"

Egg dropped his head.

"What did you do, Egg?" Carol repeated.

"I sort of called her a lady of the night."

Carol clapped a hand over her mouth and gasped. "OK, well then I suppose you can stay and sort this out." She took a step backwards out of the room. "Egg, we will have words about your manners later!"

After Carol was gone Bex turned to Egg, her eyebrows knitted. "You haven't told your mum about getting the band back together?"

"No, I've been telling her I've been at chess club and maths club. Basically all sorts of clubs I think she would approve of."

"And she doesn't suspect?"

"I think because she saw how serious I was about quitting she doesn't think anything is wrong. To be honest I never lie so why would she?" Egg shook his head. "Anyway, why are you here? I thought you hated me?"

"Yes, well, after the stuff you said I really should never speak to you again, but you're in luck! I'm a very forgiving person. I'm coming to the gig tomorrow," she announced, "if that's OK?"

"Of course it's OK."

"Nice!" Bex shifted in her seat. "Look. I came round to see you, but I also came because my dad emailed his music-industry mate with a link to your songs. Anyway, his mate loved it and asked if he could come to the gig?"

"Er, yeah, that's cool. Burt told me I have two free guests so I will put you and this guy on the list." Egg paused. "Who is he, anyway?"

Bex looked excited. "Get this! I googled him and he's the third most important person in the music industry!" she said. "I just thought, you know, my dad says you should get at least three quotes before you choose a builder! Going with the right label is important, I think."

"You're trying to create a bidding war?" Egg said with a smile.

"Something like that, I guess. Anyway his name is Jerome Clincher. Write it down."

Egg pulled a small leather-bound book from his jeans pocket, opened it and made a note.

"What's that?" Bex said pointing to the tattered book.

"It's my lyric book," Egg replied innocently

Bex eyes widened. "Cool! Is it just for your proper amazing lyrics?"

"No," he confessed. "It's my diary too."

"A diary? How very mature! Does it have anything about me in it?"

Egg blushed.

"It does. So what do you say about me in it?" Bex grinned.

He managed to meet her animated gaze. "It says you're the most attractive, soulful and intelligent person I have ever met and that I was an idiot to jeopardise our friendship with what I said to you." He dropped his eyes again.

Bex frowned a little and then stood abruptly. "I have to go.

Things to do, people to see." She extended her hand. "Friend that's a girl?" she asked.

Egg took her hand. "Friend that's a girl," he agreed with a smile.

Bex let herself out quickly and spent the walk home thinking about Egg's words. They made her smile.

SONG 9 SHOWCASE

The day of the showcase arrived and The RockAteers were ready. They had rehearsed three times a week at school and on Sunday in Burt's garage. The singer's voice was improving with every practice, the gravel in his tones measured and precise. The rhythm section was taut and tight, but with the swing and feel the songs required. Egg was the icing, his guitar style fluid and expressive. The RockAteers were in the best playing form of their lives, and Clipper's analogy, the one he had delivered at the band's final practice session before the gig, had struck a chord with them all:

"You can train till you're blue in the face, but when match day comes, you better be ready. There's nothing like the real thing to make men quake."

Inside The Borderline the buzz was electric even before the gig kicked off. The sound check, watched by twenty people, went without a hitch. Everything was ready, the names were on the guest list, the bar was stocked, the crowd had gathered outside early and The RockAteers were already in gig uniform. They looked and felt like a band.

As the four of them were led by the venue manager through a snaking corridor to the tiny dressing room, Tea marvelled at just how many band stickers adorned the walls. They covered every inch of space.

"Wow!" Clipper exclaimed when they reached the dressing room. "Look at all this beer." Two large cooler boxes were filled to the top with ice and beer bottles.

"It's not for us," Tea said in dejected tones.

"It *is*," the venue manager corrected.

"It can't be. We're all under age!" Clipper blurted out. Burt put his head in his hands and Tea groaned.

"I wouldn't know anything about that," the manager said with a half smile, before disappearing back up the corridor.

"You really are one of the biggest plebs on the face of the earth, do you know that, Clip?" Burt said.

"Sorry, mate, but I have to agree with Burt on this one," said Tea.

Clipper looked gutted for a moment. Burt spoke. "Tea, how many times do I have to tell you to call me Jack?"

"Yes, yes, all right. I'll try and remember."

Billy Visconti walked into the dressing room waving a clipboard. "Guys," he said loud enough to capture everyone's attention. "That sound check was totes amazing. You play like that in front of Wilson and you'll find yourselves on the sharp end of a record deal by the end of the night!" He tapped his clipboard with his pen. "I'm just making sure all the names you gave us for the guest list are correct."

The RockAteers nodded in unison.

"Jack, you haven't got anyone on the list? Your mum and dad aren't coming?" Billy asked looking down at the list, pen poised.

"No. They're away, and all my mates can pay full price," Burt said. "We're not a charity, right?"

"And Egg, you have Bex Vargas down, plus … Jerome Clincher, is that right?"

Billy looked up from the list. Egg nodded.

"None of my business, but … is that the same Jerome Clincher that runs Fictitious Records?"

Egg nodded again.

"Hmm," Billy said, drawing it out. "Thing is, Egg, this was supposed to be a *closed* showcase. You know, for our people. Jerome is a bit of an outsider." Billy paused again. "I just don't want you guys to be taken for a ride by someone like that."

Burt was nodding furiously. "Yes, yes, I agree with Billy. Why did you invite him, Egg?"

Egg shrugged. "I didn't know it was closed," he said. "I thought it was a proper showcase."

"Relax!" Billy said, raising a palm. "It *is* a proper showcase. It's just … it's more so our in-house team can get a sense of how great you are."

He smiled at everyone, and everyone smiled back. Except Egg.

"I should add," Billy put his hand on Egg's shoulder, "the hire of this place cost the company rather a lot of money, so, well, let's just say we want everything to be just right…" He patted the shoulder. "Don't feel bad. You weren't to know."

"Right," said Egg, woodenly.

"So can I strike his name from the list, then?" Billy said, drawing a line through the name before hearing the answer.

"Of course, Billy," said Burt. "Do it. Egg was just being dumb. Don't worry."

Billy tapped his clipboard, nodded and left the room. His face reappeared in the doorframe seconds later. "Oh yes, and you'll be getting a nice meal brought down in about half an hour. The perks of being part of the gang!"

Egg checked the time, only ten minutes to go. His stomach lurched. Clipper had been to the toilet six times in the past hour. Egg had resisted the urge, telling himself it was only nerves and that the signals telling his brain he needed to go were lies.

Bex made frequent appearances to tell the band how many people were in the venue and who had arrived. On those visits she took full advantage of the free drinks on the band's rider. Four beers and they were only the ones Egg had counted. She'd been given a backstage pass because she was going to take some live shots. Egg wondered if being drunk was conducive to taking good pictures. With only five minutes to go she burst in to the dressing room to inform them that Sir Wilson Cloom was in the building and that his large entourage included some famous faces.

Egg had been unable to confront Bex with the news that Billy Visconti had banned Jerome Clincher from the gig. He felt sure she'd be mad and he didn't want to deal with that before going on stage.

Egg studied his band mates and wondered if they were as terrified as he was. Burt was on his phone texting, looking decidedly more relaxed than the last gig they had played together. Clipper was ash white, green around the gills and mesmerised by his shoes as usual. Tea sat with his bass guitar across his lap, furiously playing, his fingers and face concentrated in one fluid act. Occasionally he would look up to take a sip of beer and smile at Egg.

"Don't look so nervous, mate. You're the best guitarist I've ever seen and you're gonna smash it tonight," the bass player said warmly.

Seconds later the venue's sound engineer came into the dressing room and announced they were on stage in one minute and it was a full house. Clipper rocketed from his seat and made for the toilet.

Burt stood up. "He better be back in time for the gig!" he said pocketing his phone, leaning into the heavily stickered mirror.

Tea stood and blew out a long stream of air. "OK then, this is it," he said, grinning at Egg. "Just think, this next hour could determine how the rest of our lives pan out!"

"I'm glad you didn't say that when Clipper was in the room," Egg said, managing a thin smile.

"Say what?" Clipper said appearing behind them, looking impossibly pale, bone-white knuckles clutching his drumsticks.

"Band prayer!" Burt ordered.

The band stepped close and took each other by the shoulders to make a tightly-packed circle of four. Heads bowed, Burt began. "Our band sent from heaven hollowed be thy name. Thine is the rock. Thine is the roll. Up The RockAteers and glory be our fame. A-fuckin'-men."

"A-fuckin'-men," the band repeated.

Burt broke away, skipped up the tunnel, whooping the words "Rock'n'roll" as he went. The rest of them followed.

146

Egg picked out Cloom and his suited posse half way through the second song, "Shop Till You Drop". They were easy to spot amongst the teenage crowd but it had taken Egg a song and a half to feel confident enough to face the audience. The tall perma-tanned man in his mid-fifties didn't move a muscle throughout the following three tracks. He didn't react to anything. Not even a nod of approval. Despite the lack of interest, The RockAteers stormed through the opening half of the set, the crowd feverish in their response. Clipper's face once again flushed with colour. Tea's warm-up paid dividends. Burt's banter and stage persona was more practised than Egg had ever seen it. After the sixth song Egg decided not to look at the music mogul any more.

Seventh in the set was "Cupid's Arrow", a song Egg thought could be a single. As soon as the opening guitar crunched, Burt was writhing around, forcing the crowd to find an even higher gear. Egg couldn't help glance at Cloom again. Still nothing. Was this man dead inside? After "Cupid's Arrow" they played "Golden", another song Egg hoped would be a single. Egg had to swap guitars for the penultimate song. It was the moment in the set when Burt had licence to freestyle with the audience.

"Anyone think they might be watching the best gig ever?"

The crowd screamed.

"I just wanted to say a huge thanks to all those who have travelled from the manor to come see us. It means a lot."

The crowd screamed some more.

"As some of you know already. Sir Wilson Cloom is in the building. We're big fans so I hope you will all make him feel very welcome."

The crowd booed.

Burt looked to his band for answers, bewilderment plastered across his face. Egg, ready with his second guitar nodded at Clipper and they plunged into "Bet On You". Burt shook his head as if to rid himself of the confusion and began to sing.

Egg glanced at Cloom again and was horrified to see that he, along with his entourage, had vanished. His heart sank. Had Burt just ruined their big chance?

It took Burt the rest of the song to regain his composure. The crowd were his again but now, he'd also noticed Cloom's disappearance. Anger flashed across his face. "You bunch of twats!" he shouted at the audience. "You've ruined every…"

Tea stepped between Burt and his microphone, buried his face into Burt's sweating mop of blonde hair and started to snarl into his ear. The venue had fallen quiet, but not quite enough for Egg to make out what Tea was saying.

Suddenly Tea stepped away and the singer grabbed the microphone once more. "Ladies and gentlemen, apologies for that slight interruption." He beamed. "What I was trying to say was that you're the most awesomest crowd we've ever had the privilege of playing in front of and we bloody love you."

Everyone cheered once more.

"This is our last song. It's called 'Satellites'." He turned expertly and nodded for the band to begin.

The RockAteers were shaken but composed enough to play the final song with precise and practised skill. The song finished and Burt gave the rapturous crowd a low bow before marching off stage.

Egg stepped out from behind the keyboard, put a limp arm up

to thank the crowd and followed his singer down the tunnel. As soon as he reached the back-stage area he stopped dead in his tracks. There in the midst of his entourage was Cloom, grinning from ear to ear.

"Great job, guys," he gushed, stepping out from his people and heading to greet Burt.

"Thanks, Sir Cloom, I hope our crowd didn't offend you by booing?"

"Water off a duck's back, my dear Jack! Am I not the modern incarnation of a pantomime villain?"

The use of Burt's stage name caused his three band mates to glance at one another in amusement.

"Guys, that was terrific! You really nailed it! Your songs really are up there! Tremendous stuff!" Billy Visconti said stepping into the circle.

"That's great you think so. We had a proper good time up there tonight and I think the fans loved it too," Burt replied beaming.

"So when are you guys gonna come in and sign the deal?" Cloom said.

"Tomorrow!" Burt blurted.

From out of nowhere Hazel crashed into the circle and flung her arms around Burt. "Oh Burtie, I love youuuuu," she gushed. "You're the great-est singer in the worrlllllllddddd."

"Get off me, you mad witch. Someone get her off me!!" Burt screamed.

A bouncer ran in and grabbed hold of Hazel. She clung onto Burt and it took some serious effort before the bouncer managed to peel her off and lead her away.

"And my name isn't Burt, you crazy biatch! It's Jack Skill," Burt shouted after her.

"Whoa there, Jackie, you may need to work on the people skills a little!" Wilson told him gravely. "The fans are important. I noticed you calling them twats earlier. At Big Tone we rarely encourage our artists to abuse the fans. A little more maturity is needed, I think, dear boy!"

"She's been stalking me for weeks, Mr Cloom," Burt said, still dripping with sweat. "She stands outside my house all the time. She scares the walking dead out of me."

Wilson gave Billy a knowing nod. "Well OK then," Wilson said. "As far as I'm concerned you boys have got yourself a deal, and I'll be seeing you all really soon."

Cloom left, his minions following close behind. Visconti remained.

"So you're going to sign with us, yes?" Billy grinned holding out his hand.

First Burt, then Tea, then Clipper and finally Egg shook his hand.

"Done deal," Visconti said. "Nice to have you on board." He winked. "Gotta split, people to do and places to be."

Egg was shaken. The usual post-gig euphoria had been replaced by anxiety and worry. He hunted for Bex in the crowd; the constant back pats and congratulatory comments hampering his search. Suddenly a warm body pressed up against his back and arms encircled him.

"Guess who," slurred the warm, husky voice.

Egg spun round beaming. "I thought you'd gone."

Bex was wearing a backless mini-dress, low cut and shimmering in the gloom of the venue.

"Wow, you changed!" Egg gulped in admiration.

"After I took the photos. By the way I think I took some really wicked pics."

"Is it made of silver?" Egg said, pointing at the tiny dress.

"Yes, it's made of silver, Egg. I'm wearing a metal dress."

"Oh, yes of course." Egg paused and gritted his teeth. He could tell Bex was pretty drunk and wondered if it might be better to tell her about Jerome in the morning.

Then he decided to get it over with. "I couldn't get Jerome Clincher into the gig."

"Yes you could. He's right over there," she said taking his hand. "Come on, I'll introduce ya."

Bex led him through the crowd; her warm palm clutching his was thrilling. Egg wished she would lead him right out of the venue and away. Three seconds later the pair stood in front of a tall, bearded man. He smiled, the creases around his eyes concertinaed, giving his face a warm, dependable look. Egg liked him immediately.

"This is Jerome Clincher," Bex said. "The mate of my dad's I was telling you about."

"I think your band rock, dude!" The man stuck out a hand.

"Thanks," Egg said bashfully.

"You two wanna drink?" he said, draining his pint glass and pointing toward the bar.

"I wouldn't mind an orange juice and lemonade," Egg nodded.

"Triple vodka and coke," said Bex.

"Not sure your dad would approve, Bee. You might look eighteen but you're not."

"OK, a double!"

"A single and think yourself lucky I'm getting you anything!"

Jerome winked at them and picked his way elegantly through the busy venue towards the bar.

"Tall man's walk," Egg mumbled as he watched him go.

"What?" Bex said leaning closer to Egg.

"He walks upright, like he's proud to be that tall. I wish I could do that."

"It's all about confidence," she said leaning closer. "He's cool, isn't he?"

"How did he get in?" Egg asked, revelling in Bex's warm, sweet, alcoholic breath on his face.

"He's a pro. He spotted his name crossed out on the guest list and took the name under it." Her lips touched his ear. "Apparently he and Wilson Cloom don't get on." Her nose brushed his cheek. "They have well different ideas about music."

Jerome returned with the drinks and Bex stepped away. The spell was broken.

"You have a natural gift for melody and that rare belief in your lyrics." Jerome said steadily. "I'm blown away that you can write with such maturity. Some of your words are really moving, man."

"I've had a hard life," Egg said with a smirk.

Bex and Jerome laughed.

152

"Can I leave you two two to it?" Bex garbled. "I wanna ... I want to go and congratulate the rest of the band."

Egg watched Bex as she slunk away, her hips navigating the crowd with intoxicating grace.

"Girlfriend?" Jerome asked.

"No," Egg replied still watching her.

"But you would like her to be?"

"Yes."

Jerome smiled warmly. "Some good material there, I bet!"

Egg nodded as he watched her disappear into the throng.

"Do you want to come in next week and see my label set-up? I think we might be able to find a place for you with us, and I think you will find it less constraining than a lot of other labels out there."

Egg shook his head sadly.

"I think I'd be wasting your time," Egg told him. "Billy Visconti has already claimed us."

"How so?"

"He asked us to sign with him and we all said yes. He shook all our hands."

Jerome's eye widened. "No, no, no, no. See now, that's exactly the reason why I hate working in this business sometimes." He studied the songwriter. "Egg, you have a gift, and that gift may well make you and some of the people around you a great deal of money. You're fifteen, right?" Egg nodded. "And you're the songwriter, right?" Egg nodded again. "Well then, you can't sign anything without your parents' consent, and besides, I advise you take your time. You don't have to trust me, but at least check out my flavour. See what I've been up to in the last ten years, the kind of acts I sign. We're totally artist focussed; there are no skeletons in my closet."

Egg listened intently but remained silent. Jerome continued.

"I know you think I'm just trying to sell myself like Billy 'Big Mouth' Visconti, and to some extent I am, but I love your band, man. I mean I think it's fresh and it's genuine and it's real. I can't promise you'll make more money with me than you would signing with Big Tone, but I can promise you'll make clean, artistic, soulful money. I got into this game to work with musicians, not to make money." He paused to take a sip of his beer. "I think you need to ask yourself whether Visconti and his puppet master, Cloom, are in the business for the same reasons."

Egg felt vindicated. His misgivings about Billy Visconti had been correct. A clash of self-satisfaction and anger boiled up inside him. "But what about the handshake? The rest of the lads are sixteen and they shook too."

"Dude, you're the songwriter, how can they sign without you? Cheeky and underhand is what that handshake was. Don't sign your life away just because you've seen Cloom on telly, and your lead singer wants fame so bad he would eat his own face to get it. Ignore the handshake. It means nothing."

"You've obviously met Jack Skill!" Egg said, marvelling at how accurately he had assessed his lead singer.

Jerome shook his head. "I haven't met him. He's the ambitious lead singer. The cliché. As soon as he walked on stage I had him pegged. Remember, man, I've been in this game twenty years."

Egg laughed, glanced over Jerome's left shoulder and spotted

Burt on the other side of the room. He was kissing someone up against the back wall of the venue. He couldn't make out who it was. A fan perhaps, or Crazel.

Moments later the pair turned.

"Bex!" he gasped, stepping past Jerome to get a better view.

He blinked and rubbed his eyes. Were they kissing? Could it really be Bex? Burt had the girl pinned again, her face hidden. His hands were all over her. The dress! It was shimmering. Egg felt sick, sicker than he had ever felt in his whole life. There was no doubt. The girl Burt was snogging was Bex!

Egg turned and fled the building.

SONG 10 SECRETS

Egg – July 26th
I should be celebrating the start of the summer,
not feeling like this. Yesterday was the last
official day of Year 11. Exams are history and I
turn sixteen in five weeks. I'm at home and it's
one in the morning. I haven't felt like writing
anything since the gig. The showcase itself was
pretty spectacular.

If this were Clipper's diary he would probably
use a football analogy to explain my night. It
was a game of two halves, first half good and
second half bad. When the drums and bass opened
for our first tune my nerves left me and I was
thrown into what Tea calls "gig zone" where
time travels quickly and all worries evaporate.
There is only the music. I wasn't thinking about
fancying Bex or worrying whether I'd messed
up my exams (which I haven't). I rehearsed so
hard for the gig that I was playing the guitar
parts in my sleep. I think the guys must have
rehearsed at home too, because we felt so rigid.
It's hard to explain but it was like a pulse,
rising and falling, with the different vibe of
each song pulling us in different directions.
It was so collectively honest. We were better
because we meant it, like the music was full
of intent and we were being our honest selves.
There was so much adrenalin flowing through us we

were performing out of our skins. It helped that the sound on stage was so brilliant and that the place was rammed full of crazy people. Our fans!

The start of the second half was pretty amazing. We pretty much got offered two record deals in one night.

Then came total and all-consuming tragedy because there on the other side of the room I saw Burt and Bex snogging. How about that for a kick in the teeth?

Why Bex? Why Bex? Why Bex? Now I can't be happy about anything. Ever.

Burt – 26th July
Five years, eight months, six days, seventeen hours and fourteen minutes. That's how long it took me to get off with Rebecca Vargas. A few shots of tequila and a couple of large cocktails helped. If only I'd known that earlier. Lol!

The kiss was spectacular and Bex defo loved it large. So what if Egg saw it? Beautiful people kiss each other all the time! That ginger fool was deluding himself if he thought he ever had a chance with someone like Bex anyway.

I can't stop thinking about her, but I have decided I'm gonna woo her gently. I don't want to scare her off.

Egg is sick as a dog, Bex is the leopard that changed her spots and I'm the cat that got the cream. #themoralofthestory #nevercountmeout

Burt was feeling a lot more confident on his second solo visit to the grand offices of Big Tone Records. After all, the deal had been verbally offered and the band had shaken on it.

This time when the beautiful receptionist came to get him from the foyer Burt was ready. He was on a roll – what the hell. They entered the lift alone and faced one another.

"So what's your name?" Burt asked, peppering her boobs with quick and obvious glances.

"Sophia," she answered, adjusting her top.

"So, Sophia, how would you like to go out for a drink with me after work?"

"How old are you?" she asked, looking surprised.

"I'm twenty. Why, how old are you?" he replied, employing the most seductive and honest smile he could muster.

"I'm nineteen." She frowned slightly. "You look younger than twenty."

"All my family look young. It's in our genes." Burt grinned and rubbed his jeans. Sophia smiled before the lift binged and the doors opened at the twentieth floor.

"I came to see you at The Borderline, you were very good!" she told him as they walked the corridor. "Hang on, how can you be twenty, I thought you were all still at school?"

"We were good, weren't we?" Burt agreed loftily. "No, not still at school. We tell people we are so they think we're younger."

"OK," she said narrowing her eyes and pouting her lips, "but I don't put out on the first date!" Burt narrowly avoided tripping over the leg of a protruding display sign. "You may as well know that right away," she added.

Before Burt could regain the power of speech they had arrived at Wilson's office. Sophia pointed to the waiting area, smiled, handed him a card and seated herself at her desk.

Burt studied the card. It had her mobile number on it. A moment later Billy Visconti was there holding out a hand.

"Shall we go in?"

"Yeah, let's."

Burt followed Billy inside the glass office.

"On your own again I see!" Wilson said.

"Er, yes … but Billy told me you guys wanted to talk to me on my own."

Wilson rocked back on his chair. "A little birdie tells me your songwriter was talking to Jerome Clincher all night," he said. "Should I be worried that The RockAteers are going back on a gentlemen's agreement?"

Burt felt a rising panic. "They were just talking! No, of course we wouldn't go back on a gentlemen's agreement."

"Good, because I'm not a man to be trifled with," he said, giving Burt a chilling look. "I hope you understand me, Mr Skill?"

"I do understand, Mr … err, Sir … Cloom, I mean sorry, Mr Sir Wilson. It's all cool. I promise."

"I'm glad to hear it. I have one more thing to ask you and then you may go." He glanced at Billy.

"Jack, you know we just want what's best for you guys, don't you?" Billy said, picking up the baton.

Burt nodded.

"Good because we do care, OK? The thing is, we feel, having seen the show, that you need to make a couple of changes."

"Changes?"

"Don't worry, Jack, it's nothing that can't be overcome together." Billy's expression switched from reassuring to solemn. "We as a company feel your drummer isn't strong enough."

An awkward silence hung in the air. "And what's the other change?" Burt asked eventually.

"Well yes, we also feel that you need a little help on the song-writing front. Nothing heavy. We feel a trip to the Song Doctor would do you the world of good."

"*Song* doctor?"

"That's what we call them, Jack," Billy said softly. "They come in and help artists become better songwriters. Hence the name 'Song Doctor'."

"So you're saying that you think our drummer's shit and our songs are so sick they need a doctor?"

Wilson, who had been watching silently from his chair, stood up, walked around his desk slowly and put a hand on Burt's shoulder.

"Calm down, Jackie. All bands go through changes. You're young and I predict many years of success ahead. Your first record needs to make the kind of impact that blows everyone else out of the water. We're talking mere tweaks, nothing more. A great drummer is the heartbeat of any band, and the songs are its life force. Both must be absolutely spot on!"

Burt shifted in his chair and looked up at Cloom. "I can do it without them," he exclaimed. "Whatever you want, I just want to get on with it." He looked across at Billy. "I just wanna be a rock'n'roll star!"

Wilson let go of Jack's shoulder and Billy relaxed.

"And you will be a rock star, but you need that songwriter of yours. He's the key. Great songs are a band's life force, remember! Imagine we combined Egg's youthful exuberance with someone who's been writing hits for years. Just think what could be achieved."

Billy stood and grinned. "We will have the papers drawn up and sent over to you to sign by the end of the week!" He paused. "Oh, and remember Egg will have to get his parents to sign his documents because he's under age."

Burt looked nervous.

"That isn't a problem, is it?"

Burt shook his head unconvincingly, stood up, reached across the desk to shake Cloom's hand and followed Billy out of the office. Cloom's voice called after them.

"Oh, and Jackie, I think you should tell your drummer sooner rather than later, don't you?"

Clipper – 31st July

Being off school on summer holidays is amazing, but George Graves is hanging around like a shit that won't flush. Sometimes he meets us after rehearsals and tries winding me up. He knows I can knock him out so now he is trying to get me with words. Like when he says stuff about other people he always adds the words poofta, homo or bumba clart. It makes me feel proper low if I'm honest, but I can't rise to it coz if I do I think I might kill him.

I have mixed emotions about the band at the moment. The showcase was wicked and proper exciting but I can't hardly sleep at night I'm so worried for everyone. Why do Burt and Egg have to argue and then not talk to each other for ages? Why can't they both just chill out? We could be blowing a wicked chance here. It's like on the footy pitch. If one of you plays badly or refuses to pass to another player then the whole team suffers.

Burt has called me and Tea to three secret meetings now. Tea said that Burt is trying to make us think how he does – like brain washing. I think he might be right. Anyway we have agreed to go and see Egg and ask why he hasn't turned up to the last two rehearsals. Burt reckons it's because Bex and him had a snog and Egg saw it, but I just can't believe Egg would chuck away everything we worked for, for something as dumb as that. So what if Bex likes Burt. What a surprise! All women like Burt. I know people say he's a proper tit but that doesn't stop him from being good-looking. Burt told us, in the last secret meeting, that he'd shagged Sophia, Sir Cloom's posh assistant, and that she was nineteen

162

and proper hot. I've cut and pasted a bunch of
emails into my blog to remind me that Burt is
mental. I've said it again and again, don't send
emails. Talk to each other – but no one listens.

From Jack Skill <jackskilz@hotmail.com >
To Michael Twining <teabag22@gmail.com >, Justin
Clipper <Justin.clipper@gmail.com >
Date 27 July 12.08

Subject: Egg Smeg

Dear Tea,

My first issue is you not taking my amp and guitar back
south. Why couldn't you just take it in the cab with the rest
of the stuff and store it at your house? I wanted to go out
after the gig.

My second issue is that Clipper is being such a sit-on-the-
fence tosser. Why can't he just pick a side?

My third issue is Egg. The fact that I'm better-looking than
him and he is in love with Bex is not my fault. It's a total
nightmare trying to keep up with his massive strops. If
Egg was a super hero he would be the Incredible Sulk.
Basically he can piss off. I cannot believe he is angry about
the other night. What for? Kissing a girl? He ran out of The
Borderline like a big girl. I know him better than you, Tea,
and he is very vindictive and enjoys being difficult. Don't
even get me started on the publishing. We need to keep
strong on that one. We deserve an equal share. What a
selfish dick he is.

I think you should speak to Egg and get him to come and apologise to me. I ruled at that gig and did an unbelievable job of convincing Wilson Cloom to sign us. Then what does Egg do? Messes it all up. #doineedtomakeitanyclearer

Jack

From Michael Twining <teabag22@gmail.com>
To Justin Clipper <Justin.clipper@gmail.com>, Jack
Skill <jackskilz@hotmail.com
Date 27 July 02:18

Subject: Re: Egg Smeg

My first issue is you're not called Jack.

My second issue is I'm not your personal slave; I'm the bassist in OUR band.

My third issue is that you think everything is all about you! It's not and the sooner you realise that the better. #nobhead What is it with all this hash-tag bollocks anyway? #inappropriateuseofhashtags #yourenotevenontwitterunob

We need to have a very honest talk about things and we need to put a plan together and work out how to stop all this internal biAtch-fighting. I think it's been proved that emails are not a good way to sort out the problems in the band. Burt – I am not sure you meant that to be a round-robin email but it was.

From Justin Clipper <Justin.clipper@gmail.com>
To Michael Twining teabag22@gmail.com>, To Jack
Skill <jackskilz@hotmail.com
Date 27 July 20:18

Subject Re: Re: Egg Smeg

Burt, you might want to check who you send your emails
to because you just sent that one about me being a "sit-
on-the-fence tosser" to me as well. I don't care what you
call me, I can ignore it. I agree with everything Tea said.

From Jack Skill <jackskilz@hotmail.com >
To Michael Twining <teabag22@gmail.com >, To
Justin Clipper <Justin.clipper@gmail.com >
Date 28 July 03.45

Subject: Re: Re: Re: Egg Smeg

Oh that's great. What a pair of bum-licking arse wranglers.
I bare my soul and tell you my most innermost problems
and you take a giant shit into my mouth. I don't
even know why I bother. And I am totally on Twitter.
#bollockstoyouboth.

From Justin Clipper <Justin.clipper@gmail.com>
To Michael Twining <teabag22@gmail.com >, To
Jack Skill <jackskilz@hotmail.com>
Date 28 July 20:18

Subject Re: Re: Re: Re: Egg Smeg

Look, Burt, this is all getting well twisted up. I think all
me and Tea are trying to do is make sure none of us say
anything we might regret on email. Let's talk face to face?

I didn't mind taking your amp home, mate. I'm sure Tea is
sorry about that. I thought about all the things you said, I
promise.

Things are tuff for us all. Let's pick ourselves up and carry
on fighting for what we know is great.

"Satellites" or "Bet On You" might become a monster hit,
and we have all these amazing people interested in us. It's
all been a distraction – maybe we should get back to just
making the music. Let's go and do what we do best and get
in the rehearsal studio and write some more good tunes?

From Michael Twining <teabag22@gmail.com>
To Justin Clipper <justin.clipper@gmail.com>, Jack
Skill <jackskilz@hotmail.com
Date 28 July 21:34

Subject: Re: Re: Re: Re: Re: Egg Smeg From:

Don't apologise for me Clipper, you tit. Burk, for the record,
I'm not sorry. But, the rest I agree with. Let's just sit down
and talk face to face. All four of us. Why are we mucking
all this up now? I refuse to work at McDonald's because 4
nearly grown men can't get on with each other.

Tea – 7th August

Me and Clipper went round to Egg's house today and he was saying he would never talk to Burt again after what he'd done. But then Clipper said he was shooting himself in the foot. It's like him and Burt are having some sort of power struggle. Burt wants us to sign with Sir Cloom and Egg wants us to go and meet with this guy called Jerome Clincher (who's signed loads of massive bands).

Egg said that even if he re-joined the band there was no way he would sign with Wilson Cloom. Clipper got all upset and reminded Egg that we had shaken on it with Billy Visconti, but Egg said that you wouldn't get a builder to come and fix something without getting at least three quotes. I think I got the point. He also said that he is still only fifteen and that he can't sign anything without his parents' consent and that his mum would rather die than see him become a full-time rock guitarist. (His mum is the scariest, gingerest woman I ever did see, but his dad looks chilled out.)

I said that I didn't see any problem with going to see this Jerome bloke. Anyway, I think I might be a genius, because I said to Egg that if I get Burt to agree to come and see this guy Jerome, then will he come back to rehearsal and stop sulking (I didn't say sulking though). Egg agreed. After we left Clipper said he should phone Bex up and get her side of the story. I don't like very many people but I reckon Clipper and me have become best mates since joining the band. He's a good lad and the only one in the band that isn't as mad as a box of maggots.

Rebecca Lopez Vargas sat on High Bench and stared out over the sprawl of London Town, dominated by the towers clustering around the pointed tip of Canary Wharf. In the near distance the grass slopes that led toward Greenwich Village shone lime-coloured in the sun. Beyond the V of the plane trees she could see the twin towers of the Queen's House, its white façade spotless and solid. It wasn't just Burt who loved this spot; Bex cherished the view from High Bench; it reassured her.

She had been too embarrassed to call Egg since the gig. If Superman's weakness was kryptonite, hers was cocktails. What was she thinking, allowing herself to be kissed by that total dickhead? All she could remember from the incident was that he had been very persistent. And he *was* charming, at least he had seemed charming in her inebriated condition. The worst thing about it was that Egg had witnessed it. She knew this because Riana had seen him storming out of the venue.

Why had she done it? She had questioned herself over and over. Eventually she concluded that she had subconsciously *wanted* Egg to see it. Because then he might actually make a move. He was so easy to talk to. She loved his quick mind. She even liked his odd sense of humour. True, he wasn't exactly what you might describe as fit, but if all good-looking boys were anything like the ones she'd come across so far – like Burt – then she wouldn't be spending too much time with any of them.

Just then she spotted Egg as he came trudging up the slope towards her, his eyes fixed on the terrain ahead. By the time he got to the top, he was panting.

"Late night?" she enquired, with a reserved smile.

"I haven't been sleeping that well to be honest." He sat down on the bench next to her and looked out at the view.

"Look, Egg, you must be wondering why I have called you up here. I'll get straight to the point."

"Please do."

"OK … well … not that it's any of your business, but … I hate myself for … kissing Burt like I did, and … if I could turn the clock back I'd erase it. You get me? I do mess shit up when I'm pissed. I don't know what happens."

There was a long silence before Egg spoke. "You're right, it is none of my business."

"OK," she shrugged, looking down at her lap. "Well … if that's true, why did you run out of the venue all angry and stuff and haven't rung me back all week?"

Bex could see he was blushing.

"Dunno," he managed, clearly unable to look at her.

She pursed her lips and chose her words carefully. "Is it because you're head-over-heels in love with me and you absolutely can't bear seeing me kissing another boy?"

"No!" Egg exclaimed, louder than he had meant to.

"OK then, so why haven't you called me back then?" she asked quietly. "I thought we were friends!"

"I said I dunno, and I don't."

"OK, but can we go back to being friends? I hate all this."

Egg let out a long sigh and nodded.

"So tell me what's going on with… " – she paused for dramatic effect – "The *RockAteers*?"

Egg rolled his eyes and sniffed. "Burt is trying to make us sign a deal with Sir Wilson Cloom but I'm not old enough to sign it without my parents' permission, and anyway, I'd like to see what your dad's mate Jerome has to say."

"So, go and see him, Egg. You've got as much say as Burt. Don't let that fool bully you into signing with someone you're not sure about."

For the first time Egg turned to face her. Their eyes met. A smile flashed across his face but just as suddenly it dropped. He frowned and returned his gaze across to London.

"You just saw me kissing Burt, didn't you?" she said.

"Look, I've gotta go." Egg stood up and started to make his way back slowly down the slope. Bex watched him until he disappeared through the wrought-iron gates at the bottom of the hill.

Burt – 9th August
So, they all turn up to rehearsal and they have
obviously hatched this plot against me, because
they already know what each other is going to
say. So they want to go to see this bloke called
Jerome. So I say, and this is a really good point:

"Why do we need to go see the 3rd most important
person in the industry when we have the 1st most
important person in the industry wanting to sign
us?"

And what was Egg's argument? Builders! What have
bloody builders got to do with anything? People,
even my so-called mates, go on about how clever
they think Egg is and that he has really changed

since he started wearing cool clothes, but all
I see is a lanky ginger tit! Who asked him to
be in the band in the first place? Me that's
who! Also who paid for all his new clobber and
contact lenses and stuff? I did. He thinks I don't
know that him and Bex used my card for his new
wardrobe. You ever heard of a bank statement, Egg?

And another thing. How am I going to convince
them we have to get rid of Clipper? Billy's rung
me twice since I went into the office last week.
I'm going to have to call an emergency meeting
with me, Egg and Tea.

Also, why the hell is Bex not answering any of
my phone calls? This is a circle of absolute
bollocks. Bex doesn't call me back and suddenly
Crazel is at my door and I felt lonely so I
shagged her. She hasn't mentioned me screaming
at her after the gig the other week. It always
makes me feel worse after she leaves. I shouldn't
be doing it. I still think Crazel has a really fit
body.

She actually showed me on the computer what she
gets up to for the band the other day. She really
has done a tonne of stuff for us. If it wasn't for
the amazing music she wouldn't have done anything,
but I think she does help. Like all the forums she
goes on, talking to people about the band and all
the social networks she is always posting comments
on. The only problem really is that she is properly
in love with me, and of course as soon as I get
over whatever's bugging me she will have to go.

Now it's all come to a bit of a head because
this girl I met at Wilson's office came back

to my house the other day and we had sex. Talk about fit! Sophia is like honey on toast with trickle on top. I could rubberneck her unbelievable fitness for days.

If I am completely honest Crazel is probably more fun than Sophia even though Crazel is a six out of ten and Sophia is a nine. Of course Bex is a ten out of ten.

Anyway Crazel must have smelt Sophia on my pillow because she said. "Oh, another girl has been in our bed." I said it was my bloody bed not ours and then she started crying. She didn't have a go at me or anything. I did feel bad.

Tea – 14th August
Burt asked me and Egg to meet up with him in Greenwich on this bench he calls High Bench. Basically its high and it's a bench. #reallyimaginativeburt. #thatswhyyoudontwritethesongs

I recorded the conversation on my phone like some sort of Sherlock Holmes because I believe Jack Tit Balls Windsor is a slippery bastard and I sensed something bad was coming. I'm glad I did.

BURT – *As you know I went to see Billy Visconti and Wilson Cloom last week.*
ME – *Was that when you pulled his secretary?*
BURT – *Yes, but that's not important. They told me they thought we were amazing and that I was*

*an amazing front man and that you were both
good too.*
ME – *How nice of them.*
BURT – *Can I carry on, please? Basically they
want to sign us, and I think we'd be mad not to.
I also think that because I started the band I
should be listened to properly.*
EGG – *It takes more than one person to start
a band, Burt, look up the word band in a
dictionary.*
BURT – *Yes, but I was the one that got it all
together. Do you get me? Anyway will you just
let me get what I have to say out, please? Billy
and Wilson think that we should ditch Clipper and
look for another drummer!*

Me and Egg stared at him for ages.

EGG – *For what reason?*
BURT – *They think he's not tight enough and a bit
fat.*
EGG – *Well that's not true, he is good enough and
isn't at all fat.*
BURT – *Why do you always disagree with everything
I say?*
EGG – *Because, Burt, you speak horse manure 99.9%
of the time.*
BURT – *What do you think, Tea?*
ME – *I think Egg's being generous. I think you
speak horse shizzle 100% of the time.*
BURT – *Not about that! I mean what do you think
about Clipper leaving the band?*
ME – *I think you're talking about him being
booted out of the band, not him leaving of his
own free will! I agree with Egg, and I think he's
a great drummer. So what if he is a bit on the
chunky side.*
BURT – *Look lads, I admire your loyalty but*

173

image is everything in this day and age. He just doesn't fit in. Besides how's it going to look having a gay drummer? Don't get me wrong. I'm not a misogynist. I have loads of gay friends, but rock'n'roll bands never have gay people in them.

TEA – What are you trying to say?

BURT – Oh come on, you telling me you didn't know he was gay?

EGG – Burt, I'm going to pretend you didn't say that. Firstly I want to go back to the point I made earlier about you speaking rubbish 99.9% of the time. I think your last comments perfectly encapsulate this.

BURT – La de da. Big words might break my bones but bullshit will never hurt me. Bang off in your face.

Burt held his palm up to Egg's face. Egg looked really angry.

EGG – I don't know what you're talking about Burt! But I do know that you have exactly zero gay friends and that you are being blatantly homophobic and at this precise moment not in the slightest bit misogynistic, although given half a chance I feel sure you would give womankind a rough ride.

BURT – Damn right I'd give womankind a rough ride. I'd give all the ladies a rough ride all night long.

EGG – There you are! That's misogyny, Burt. Well done and thank you ever so much for being so implausibly predictable. Look – I really don't want to be here anymore, so I'm going. Before I do, we are going to see Jerome Clincher next week. If he also thinks we need a new drummer then maybe we'll talk again, but that decision will be based on his abilities and not his sexual orientation.

As far as I'm concerned it's all for one and one for all. It's the only way it can work.

Egg got up and left.

ME – *How do you know he's gay?*
BURT – *Because it's obvious that he fancies me and I'm a boy and that's gay.*
ME – *You think everyone fancies you.*
BURT – *I don't think you fancy me.*
ME – *You're damn right I don't fancy you. I don't fancy any men.*
BURT – *So you agree that we should boot him out of the band?*
ME – *No, I didn't say that. I don't know what I think.*
BURT – *Well you better decide fast or we might miss our big chance.*

I'm not sure where it came from but I just decided right there and then that Clipper was brilliant and even if he was gay, he was the closest thing I had to a best mate. He was a well good laugh and a great drummer.

ME – *OK. I've decided. I agree with Egg!*
BURT – *You know what, Tea? You really are dumb.*
ME – *You know what, Burt? You really are a back-stabbing bastard.*

I got up from the bench and started walking down the hill. I only got about twenty metres before Burt shouted at me (you can actually hear it faintly on the recording because I didn't stop recording till I got out of the park).

BURT – *And they want us to go see a song doctor, so your bum chum, Egg, isn't that amazing after all.*

That's when I stuck my finger in the air and gave him the big bird. It's my seventeenth birthday tomorrow. Thanks for that present, Burt! Nice work. Bang off in your face more like!

SONG 11 CHANGES

Within ten years and by the age of thirty-five, Jerome Clincher had risen from a junior A&R position to Managing Director of Fictitious Records. After his promotion to MD he signed three acts, one after the other. All three became global success stories and Fictitious became the hottest label in the country.

Jerome knew it was going to be difficult to lure The RockAteers from the big bucks of Wilson Cloom. One thing was for sure; he wouldn't lie or try to tempt the band with hollow promises. Being in a working band was tough and not for the faint-hearted. He decided his first job was to tell them what they were letting themselves in for.

His phone buzzed, and the receptionist informed him that the band were downstairs in the lobby. He got up from his desk slowly and smiled at his colleague opposite.

"Good luck," she said, smiling back.

"Fingers crossed," he acknowledged with a nod.

He made his way into the partitioned conference room and positioned himself at the head of the oak table. A moment later the four youngsters entered.

First through the door was the singer, tall and handsome, with an air of arrogance. Jerome believed ego was an essential trait in a singer. Then the bassist, olive-skinned and almost as handsome as the singer, the difference being that the bassist seemed to have no clue about his obvious good looks. As a player he was solid as a rock, Jerome had noted at the gig – dependable and steadfast. He had liked the way the kid stood on stage, loose and cool, his bass guitar low on his hip.

Egg followed the bassist. He was the most versatile and original guitarist Jerome had seen in years. He might not have as much confidence as the singer but he was also the best songwriter of any age he'd heard in a decade of working in the industry.

The drummer strolled in last and the quartet was complete. The sticks man was totally different again, thick-set and excitable, smiling amiably. Everyone would warm to this guy right away. His on-stage persona was brilliant too, singing along to the songs, diving around the kit in the style of The Who's Keith Moon.

After the introductions, Jerome kicked off. "I hope you don't mind, but I rang a couple of pals and asked them if they would give your music a listen … and I'm going to start name-dropping in about two seconds."

The band laughed.

"Cab Jones from The Desert Kings rang me back and raved about your song 'Love and War' for about ten minutes; said it reminded him of a poppy Neil Young. And Sergio from Krakatoa emailed me saying that 'The RockAteers are the future'. He really loved it. Both told me they would like to have you out on tour with them next year."

Clipper put his hand up.

"Why are you putting your hand up, Clipper? I'm not a teacher," Jerome said with a smile.

"Do *you* think I should be replaced?" he asked impassively.

The rest of the band stared at Clipper in shock. Jerome also seemed surprised.

"No, I don't, Clipper. Why do you ask?"

"Well because … you see … I read Tea's blog the other day…" Clipper flashed a harsh look at Burt, who was staring at the floor.

"I see," said Jerome.

"Yeah, and the lads had a meeting because Sir Cloom doesn't think I'm a good enough drummer." Clipper's anger was starting to show. "And Burt thinks me being gay is a problem!"

"So you *are* gay?" Tea exclaimed. "Hang on. How did you read my blog?"

Clipper folded his arms, fell silent, ignored his band mates and sat looking at Jerome. Jerome looked from one to the other. Eventually he broke the silence.

"OK, guys. Look, firstly I want to tell you that I think you're all fantastic. It's important that you realise that Wilson Cloom is one of the finest operators in the business, and he is known for his ferocious desire to get what he wants. If Jack has been manipulated and been given a list of demands, and I am not saying he has, then it just goes to show, once again, what a smooth operator Wilson is, and just how good you guys are. Now, Jack…" Jerome looked at Burt. Burt's chin remained firmly on his chest.

"…I get the impression you're ambitious and that's exactly what I want from a singer; that and a great singing voice, and you certainly have that. Clipper…" Jerome turned his gaze on

Clipper, who stared back, the hurt still visible, "…I think you're a great drummer, dude, and no, I don't think you need replacing. Look, guys, you shouldn't rush into anything. In fact I have never seen a band more in need of a manager, or someone that can be a bridge between you all. You're all fifteen, remember, why the…"

"I was seventeen last week," Tea interrupted. "I'm in the year above the rest of the lads."

"Happy Birthday, Tea. OK, so you're all fifteen apart from Tea, is that right?"

"I'm sixteen," said Clipper.

"So am I," Burt said, sounding sulky.

"OK… What about you Egg?"

"Yes, I am fifteen, sixteen in a week."

"Right, so you would have to wait to sign the deal until then anyway. Unless you think your parents would sign the contracts for you?"

Jerome noted Burt's look of annoyance.

"What I was going to say is: why the big rush? You proba-bly think it's normal to have all these top record execs running around after you, but only a very small percentage of bands get any interest from A&R people at all, let alone actual offers…"

"Do you like our name?" Tea butted in again.

"Your *name*? Er, to be honest, no, I think it's pretty awful. But – maybe that's exactly what will make it good."

"See, I told you it was shit," Tea told Burt. Burt didn't look up, his eyes were closed, and he seemed to be in pain.

"You guys are missing my point. What I'm saying is: enjoy being in a band, just enjoy being together, writing great songs and playing to screaming fans. Don't get lost in all the politics."

"You haven't answered my question about me being gay," said Clipper.

"Of course it's not important," Jerome said. "As you get older you'll find out that no one cares if you're gay. All that stuff is immaterial."

"So, do you want to offer us a deal, then?" Tea said.

"Hmm, I did before you all walked in. If I'm honest, nothing would have made me happier. However, on reflection, I think you're not quite ready. I'd like to see if you can last a month before I table anything. Signing a band is a huge risk, a huge investment. I really need you to be solid and firing on all cylinders."

"So that decides it, we sign with Wilson Cloom!" Burt exclaimed, finally looking up.

Before Jerome could react to this, Egg spoke. "No, Burt, we are *not* going to sign with Sir Wilson Cloom. Haven't you listened to anything Jerome has being saying? For a start I can't sign a deal till I'm sixteen," he said in a low hiss. "Seriously all this has turned you mental. We need to have some rules. We can't talk behind each others' backs any more, for example. We do need a manager, we need to start being a band again, not a bunch of headless chickens."

Egg paused and looked at Jerome. "Would you chair a vote for us, please?"

Jerome looked truly taken aback. "Yes, I suppose so!" he said.

"Right! I am going to humour you, Burt. Hands up those who want to sign this deal with Wilson Cloom as soon as possible."

Slowly, Burt raised his hand.

"OK, hands up who wants to get back to being a band and forget all this 'getting signed' business? With our gay drummer bashing away behind us all the way," Egg said, raising his hand with a smirk.

"Cheeky git!" Clipper exclaimed before putting his arm up.

Tea raised his hand and the three of them turned towards Burt.

"All right, all right! You win. We don't sign with Wilson Cloom, and we go back to being a band." He stood up and wandered over to the window. "But can everyone stop being a dickhead? It's really wearing me out!"

Egg – 22nd August

Eleven straight A's. In your face, Mum. It was a bit weird picking up my exam results with Clipper today. He wasn't nervous at all, despite getting six D's an E and an F. He seemed stunned that a person was allowed to take eleven GCSE's let alone get that many A's. He got bad grades but didn't care; I got good grades and really cared. I knew it would give me my freedom. He only looked sad when I asked him about what he was going to do about his place on the Charlton football team. He told me he hasn't told his dad yet.

I've been seeing a lot of Bex since we had our heart to heart on High Bench. I wrote a song about her. I've started to write good stuff again now the band's running smooth again and Burt has stopped acting like a lunatic. Jerome has rung me every few days since our meeting to ask how things are going. He helped put us in touch with a good lawyer and a great management company.

This bloke called Harry seems like the best contender. It's funny, Jerome told us that Cab from the Desert Kings and Sergio from Krakatoa had listened to our music, but it got lost with what went down after. But it's so brilliant those dudes dig our stuff (I hope Thom from Radiohead digs it too). I can't even begin to imagine what it would be like to tour with either of those bands. The Desert Kings are amazing.

I'm confused about Bex and her feelings toward me. Sometimes I think she might fancy me, but other times she goes on about other boys and tells me I'm like a thirty year old. I absolutely can't find the confidence to kiss her so I've decided to play her the song I wrote about her. It's called "Sovereign". I felt in a cheesy kind of romantic mood. I hope she doesn't think that I think she loves me; that would be disastrous. I mean it's only loosely based on her… Who am I kidding? Every song I've written in the last year has been about her. I think she might totally be my muse.

Sovereign

Wake me up before you fly, dry my bones and wipe my eyes
Take my hell and move it over there
Meet my heart and tell me true
What would I do with or without you
There's something in the way that she loves me
There's something in the way that she moves me
I won't beg and I won't borrow, I won't steal a single thing
You could be my sovereign and I could be your king

Sir Wilson Cloom glowered at his computer screen.

> **From: The RockAteers [:<u>therockateers@gmail.com</u>]**
> **To: William Visconti <<u>billy.visconti@bigtonerecords.com</u>>**
> **FW: Wilson Cloom [:<u>wilson.cloom@bigtonerecords.com</u>]**
> **Date 30 August 08:08**
>
> **Subject: FW: Re: Sorry**
>
> FYI, sorry boss...
>
> Dear Billy Visconti,
>
> I'm really sorry but I'm afraid we can't sign with your company. Please tell Sir Wilson we are all very sorry and thank you for being interested in us.
>
> Jack "Burt" Skill.

Wilson leaned back in his chair and stared out the window, raging beneath the controlled exterior. Only one thing would satisfy him, and that was revenge. He swivelled back to his desk and hit the talk button on the intercom.

"Sophia, get in here. Now."

Within moments the young assistant was standing in front of him, concern etched on her face.

"Jack Skill?"

Sophia nodded warily. "The boy I fetched up here a couple of times you mean, Sir?"

"Don't play the innocent with me, young lady. I know you've been fraternising with him."

Sophia reddened. "I only kissed him."

"Sit down."

The girl complied, crossing both her arms and long tanned legs.

"I need you to do something for me. I want you to call Jack and I want you to start seeing him again."

Surprise registered on the girl's face and Cloom's lips creased slightly.

"Don't worry. You won't be breaking the law. He is sixteen!"

Sophia gave her boss a look of bewilderment. "But … he told me he was twenty!"

Cloom burst into laughter. "He looks barely out of nappies. I won't believe for a moment you thought he was twenty years old. I asked Billy to find out when he was born in case we had trouble signing a minor, so I can assure you he is not twenty."

"But… Really. I didn't know! I promise!"

"I believe you. Thousands wouldn't. Let's get back to the matter at hand. I want you to gain his trust and tell me what the band is planning to do, who they intend to sign with, that sort of thing."

"You want me to spy on him?"

"I'll make it worth your while. Assuming you come up with the goods."

Sophia closed her eyes, and nodded once, sharply.

"And Sophia … don't make it too obvious, will you?" Wilson nearly smiled. "OK, well, see what you can come up with."

He waved his arm. Sophia got the message and started to walk towards the door.

"Oh, and Sophia," he added, stopping her in her tracks. "Type up the usual 'dismissal' letter for me to sign, will you?"

"Certainly, Sir." She paused, with one foot out of the door. "Who should I address it to?"

"Billy Visconti."

Egg practised his new song until his calloused fingertips began to bleed and his voice had developed the kind of gravelly huskiness singers would pay good money to acquire. What if she didn't like it? What if she felt uncomfortable with the romantic overtones? They were supposed to be friends. Singing her this song was like giving her a love poem. And what about the sentiment? "Something in the way she loves me." How presumptuous and egotistical. Even if she did love him, shouldn't he write "something in the way I love her"? But that wasn't the song. He had tried it that way and it didn't make sense.

Egg had arranged to meet her on High Bench later on that day. Somehow he had to find the courage to take his guitar up to High Bench and sing her the song. It was about time he told her how he felt. He had to conquer the fear.

Egg placed his acoustic guitar on its stand and sat on the edge of his bed in the tiny bedroom. He made a decision. It was the same one he had made all day and then reversed. He would not sing her the song. A minute later he reached over, picked up his guitar and started strumming the chords again.

Burt grabbed his jacket and turned towards the huge hall mirror. His hair was looking flat. The new product the salon had sold him wasn't working. He scrunched his long fringe to try and inject more volume, clenched his jaw and winked at his reflection.

"You really are a poser!" the voice sneered.

Burt jumped, a lump forming in his throat as he registered the figure suddenly beside him.

His father was leaning casually on the door frame; the glossy silvering hair and slick tailored suit a seriously unwelcome surprise. Burt would be forever struck by how similar in shape, size and look he and his dad were. They were almost identical. It was like looking at himself in thirty years. Burt shivered at the thought.

"What are you doing back?" Burt asked nervously.

A fleeting look of uncertainty swept over his father's face; an unreadable chink in the armour. "I live here, Burt. I pay your bills, I pay for your food and I pay for your babysitters," his father said, taking a long drag on his cigarillo before blowing the smoke into Burt's face.

Burt made for the door, but his father took a step sideways and barred the way.

"So what's all this rubbish your sister tells me? You're in a band?"

"It's not rubbish, we're good and we're gonna make stacks of cash!" Burt replied defiantly, attempting to squeeze past his dad.

Richard Windsor released a burst of mocking laughter. "You're delusional! Just like your mother," he said, catching Burt by the collar of his jacket.

Burt gripped his father's wrist. "Let me go, please, just let me go," he cried.

His father pushed the lit end of the Café Creme close to Burt's face. "How about we end your musical career before it gets started, pretty boy? No such thing as a disfigured lead singer."

Burt twisted and yanked himself free. "You will never amount to anything!" He heard as he fled upstairs.

Burt – 1st September
My dad came home yesterday. He wasn't supposed to be back for weeks. He really is one evil piece of shit. I was bloody elated to find him gone the next day. I will show that evil bastard I can make something of myself. I'm gonna be in the biggest rock band in the world and Bex will be my wife and we are gonna be twenty times richer than him and we are gonna have beautiful children together and he ain't gonna be allowed to go anywhere near them.

Bex sat on High Bench, her eyes fixed on the gates at the bottom of the hill. She was always the first to arrive. She liked to watch the tall auburn figure of Egg walk up the hill; getting closer and closer, as he hiked up the steep slope. She was excited. He had told her on the phone he had a surprise for her.

She had seen a real change in him since he had faced Burt down over the whole Clipper thing. Whether it was a new found confidence or because he was more comfortable in her company she wasn't sure. She didn't really care. He also seemed to have forgiven her for her mistake with Burt. They never talked about it and Bex was glad of that. She made a point of being as distant from Burt as possible. When Burt tried to engage her, she would withdraw and often totally ignore him. It was her relationship with Egg that she cherished – more and more with every passing day.

They talked about everything now. He told her his fears and dreams and she told him hers. They had a game, a test of personal knowledge. They fired questions at each other like "what was the date and exact time I was born?" and "what is my maternal grandmother's name?" They were fanatical in learning of one another's details.

Bex beamed when she saw Egg amble into the park. She couldn't help it. She always smiled when she saw him. He was carrying his guitar. Was that something to do with the surprise?

"They're planning on signing to Fictitious Records," Sophia announced. "Jack told me they're going on tour with The Desert Kings next year. He doesn't stop going on about it."

Sir Wilson Cloom studied his employee for a long time before answering. "We might make a junior A&R girl out of you yet," he mused, a crooked smile flickering on his pinched lips. "OK, now you've completed that job I want you to start feeding him suggestions."

"Suggestions?"

"Hint at stuff … tell him he should sign with Big Tone as a solo act." He paused. "But this is the most important thing I want you to say … tell him that you heard on the grapevine that Jerome Clincher is a liar and that he is renowned for promising bands the world and not delivering. Got it?"

"But, Sir," Sophia pleaded. "I got all the information you asked for. Please don't make me do this any more. It doesn't feel right."

Cloom leaned forward on his elbows and made a steeple with his fingers. "A little longer, my dear," he said, staring at her with cold eyes. "You will disappoint me if you don't finish the job. You wouldn't want to do that would you?"

Wilson gave the usual dismissive hand-gesture and watched as she scuttled out of the room.

Once she'd gone, he swivelled ninety degrees in his chair and looked out across London. He needed to consider his next move carefully. Should he call Jerome's boss? Fictitious Records was part of a bigger umbrella company, and Wilson knew the top dog there pretty well. That would be the quickest route to kybosh

The RockAteers' chances of being signed by Fictitious. But then again, would Jerome's boss be threatened enough by Sir Wilson or would he side with his star centre-forward? Cloom had to concede that Jerome was a popular man and he certainly had the Midas touch when it came to spotting talent. No, he decided, it was too risky.

Suddenly his eyes brightened. He picked up the phone and dialled. "Get me Hans Molander. Tell him it's Wilson Cloom."

Hans Molander was the head of one of the largest concert promoters in the world, a far subtler instrument for Wilson to exploit. His company staged shows for the biggest acts around the globe, and many of those artists were on Wilson's label. Hans Molander made millions from his custom. If there was anyone who couldn't afford to cross Sir Wilson Cloom, it was Hans.

"Wilson, how are you?" came the familiar Swedish accent.

"I'm well, thanks. Hans, as always I'm in a rush. I need to ask you a favour."

"How can I be of service?"

"I need you to call The Desert Kings Live agent and tell them not to allow The RockAteers to support them on their next tour."

There was a lengthy silence, followed by a quite audible sigh. "This is a big favour you ask, Wilson! The word on the street is that the band you speak of … The RockAteers … they're going to blow up. I can't afford to make enemies out of new bands. They will one day sell out the stadiums I book."

Wilson played his ace. It was the only card he needed. "You can't afford to make an enemy of me either, now can you, Hans? You don't think I'd have asked if it wasn't important."

There was a new note of alarm in Hans's voice. "Wilson! What are you saying, old friend? This is very serious things you are saying to me!"

"I realise that, Hans. The gravity of the situation is evident simply by the fact I ask." Wilson pulled the trigger. "The bottom line is, Hans, can I count on your support? Or not?"

The line fell silent.

"Of course you can count on me," Hans said finally. "Look," he said. "I need to think about this, can you give me a couple of hours?"

Egg couldn't work out how she did it. No matter how early he arrived, Bex would always be on High Bench before him. He always felt awkward walking up the hill with her watching. He'd always hated the way he walked. Now it was being scrutinized by the girl he so badly wanted to impress.

The first time he looked up from the ground was when he arrived at the summit and put his guitar case down.

"That hill never fails to break me," he said with a grin.

"I suggest more cardio in that exercise regime of yours!" she replied beaming.

He sat down next to her on the bench, leaned over and kissed her lightly on the cheek. Whenever Egg used to greet Bex he would nod a shy hello. A week ago there had been a break-through. Now whenever they met he would give her a peck on her cheek. He loved it.

"OK, I've got a great question for the Egg 'n' Bex quiz," she said. "It's still thirty all but I think I'll go one up here."

"Go for it, but I doubt you can beat … 'The Brain'. It's just too massive."

"OK, what date did we first meet and what was the first thing I ever said to you?"

"Before I answer that I need to get a rule check. This is worth two points, right?"

Bex frowned and shook her head. "No way! One point. It happened all at the same time."

"You're such a cheat. OK, let me see…" Egg squeezed the bridge of his nose and narrowed his eyes as if in deep concentration. "It was September 26th and you introduced yourself and told me I could play that thing. That thing being my guitar. I remember it very well because I was unable to answer you back. I was mortified."

"Correct!" Bex said leaning into his shoulder with a friendly nudge. "And for a bonus point can you tell me why you couldn't reply?"

Egg looked at her for a long moment. She smiled back.

"I wrote you a song!" Egg said eventually, breaking eye contact.

"Great!" Bex said with a disappointed sigh, shuffling up the bench and settling away from him a little.

Egg picked up the guitar and gulped. He closed his eyes and began to strum. "I hope you like it," he muttered before he started to sing.

When he finished, Egg opened his eyes and looked over at

Bex. His heart sank. She wasn't in tears or beaming with wonder. In fact, she didn't look that impressed at all.

"You didn't like it?" he said dejectedly.

Bex shook her head impatiently. "It was nice."

"I wrote it for you."

"Thank you."

Egg put his guitar back in its case and wished the ground would swallow him up.

Bex put her hand on his hand. "Egg," she whispered moving back up the bench toward him. "Tell me why you couldn't talk to me that first day we met."

Egg turned but couldn't meet her eyes. "Because you didn't know I existed and I've been in love with you since the first time I saw you."

He looked up and saw Bex had moved closer, her green eyes twinkling, her lips parted in a warm smile. He leaned in and suddenly his lips were on hers. The thrill was almost too much. His neck hairs bristled and his head buzzed with a million fizzing sparklers and his body began to respond. Egg didn't care. The sensation was too potent to stop through embarrassment. It was the old, timid Egg who would have panicked. This kiss was the single most important thing that had ever happened to him. He reached up and cupped his hand behind her head, letting her thick, glossy hair run through his fingers. She pressed harder with her mouth, her body pushing closer with every heartbeat. Finally Bex drew away and took a long, deep breath. She smiled the most extraordinary smile, and Egg knew his life would never be the same again.

Egg – 2nd September
I'm not sure if the pages of this diary will believe what happened last night! I'm struggling to believe it myself. I went to meet Bex on High Bench and I played her the song I wrote for her. She didn't care about the song and kept asking me why I couldn't talk to her when I first met her. So I told her and bang, we kissed. We properly kissed! And then we couldn't stop kissing and it was the most incredible feeling in the whole world ever. Now I know where cloud nine is and I want to be on it forever!

Clipper – 2nd September
I told my dad I didn't want to join Charlton Youth team today. He just looked devastated and didn't say anything. I don't really know what to do now. I know I've really let him down. How can I tell him I'm gay on top of that? My mum said that because I got bad exam results she really worries because if I'm not going to be a footballer then what am I going to do? I told her I was gonna be in a big rock band but she wasn't impressed. I also told her that Burt got 8 U's in his exams; I thought it would make my terrible results look better but she didn't think so.

 Things with the band have sort of got back to normal now. No one really mentions the whole "me being gay" thing or that Burt tried to get me booted out of the band. At rehearsal yesterday Egg couldn't stop grinning. I asked him why he was so happy, and he said him and Bex had started going out. He said it was all a massive secret and I couldn't tell anyone. I was happy for him but then I thought, damn! We have just got back to normal and now Egg is seeing the girl Burt is obsessed with.

Egg played us his new songs yesterday and they are proper brilliant. He also asked us if we thought it might be time to talk to labels again. I think he wants to sign with Fictitious now. I know they're keen to sign us so why not. Since the meeting with Jerome, Egg has sort of become more of the leader. Surprisingly Burt seems cool with it. I think he eventually got what Jerome was saying. Plus Burt absolutely loves the Desert Kings, and I reckon the fact that we are going on tour with them is making him behave himself. Or maybe it's about birds. He told me yesterday that Sophia and him are going out properly now. Hopefully that will make him less crazy when he eventually finds out about Egg and Bex.

SONG 12 REVELATIONS

Burt could smell her perfume as soon as he stepped inside the house. First his father, now what was his mother doing here? Whose was the Range Rover parked in his drive with the strange guy in the driver's seat? He ignored the entrance-hall mirror and made for the kitchen.

As soon as he entered the room he knew all was not well. Millie sat staring miserably down at the kitchen table. Next to her sat the willowy figure of his mother, smoking a thin, white, American cigarette. Claudia Windsor didn't turn to acknowledge her son.

"Burt!" Millie cried out. She tore across the room and flung her arms around him.

"What's going on?" he demanded, as he lifted his sister off the floor and hugged her close to him.

"Mum's sending me away, to boarding school in Scotland and I don't want to go. Please don't let them! Please, Burt! I just want to stay here with you. I don't want to go there. Please!"

"What?" Burt said, staring at his mother.

She turned her perfect features toward him, completely impassive to her daughter's increasing sobs. Her immaculate blonde pony-tail, blood-red Chanel manicure and sleek black Vivienne Westwood dress accentuated the polished chill of her demeanour.

"I know she's been living here with you, Burt. Don't try and lie to me."

"I wasn't gonna lie. So what if she's living here? It's her home! Grandma's useless. I look after her. You're never here. What do you care?"

"I care a great deal, James. I'm her mother."

Millie began to cry uncontrollably into the crook of Burt's neck. She was too heavy for him, but he held fast, hugging her with every ounce of strength he could muster.

Suddenly he spotted the large capsule suitcase parked by the door.

"What's that?" he asked.

"I wasn't keen, but she insisted we wait and say goodbye," Claudia replied.

"What do you mean?" Burt gulped, feeling his bottom lip begin to tremble.

"The school have agreed to take her early. I have to be in Dubai on Thursday."

"Don't let her take me, Burt," Millie sobbed, her hair plastered to her tear-streaked face. She turned to her mother. "I don't want to go to that school and I don't want to go ANYWHERE with YOU! I want to be with BURT!"

"That's enough, Amelie," her mother barked, storming over and attempting to prize them apart. "You will love it once you're there. I boarded from the age of seven. You're nearly ten!" She tried to tear her daughter's hand from her son's neck but Millie held fast. "We're spending thousands. Now LET go. We have to leave."

Burt twisted away from his mother. "Just get out, Claudia! She isn't going anywhere," he screamed, holding Millie as tightly as he could.

"I thought you might get clingy. You were clingy as a boy," she sneered, coolly retrieving her mobile phone from the kitchen table. She held the phone to her ear. "You can come in and give me a hand now."

Moments later the man Burt had seen in the driveway was inside the kitchen. The alien presence caused Burt to shake with fury.

"Get out!" he screamed. "Leave us alone."

The big man looked towards his mother for instruction.

"I'll bring her luggage if you can bring her," she said officiously, before taking hold of the suitcase and wheeling it from the room.

The driver took a step toward Burt and Millie, towering over Burt by at least six inches, well muscled under his light sports jacket. The salt and pepper stubble gave him an almost wolf-like quality.

"You lay one hand on us and I will kill you," Burt muttered through clenched teeth, staring him down.

The man put a hand on Burt's neck and squeezed, Burt shrieked in pain. He let go of his sister and fell onto the kitchen floor clutching his shoulder. Millie kicked out but the driver was too quick. He gathered her up roughly and followed Burt's mother out of the kitchen. Burt scrambled to his feet and bolted after them. Just before they reached the front door Burt flew at the driver's back. It was as if he had hit a human wall. He flew back-

199

wards against the hallway mirror, hitting the back of his head hard, and slumped to the floor.

Burt watched as his sister was dragged from the house. He shook his head, got to his feet and raced down the steps. Millie was being wrestled into the Range Rover, kicking and screaming. Burt sprinted across the gravel, but he was too late. The door closed just as he reached the four by four. He screamed and thumped his hands against the windows, his sister's face on the other side distorted in agony.

Suddenly the car was moving, speeding out of the drive. Burt chased after it onto the road, his eyes fixed on the rear window and Millie's tear-streaked face staring back at him. The car sped around the bend and out of sight. Exhausted, he stopped, sat down cross-legged on the pavement and began to sob.

Burt – 2nd September
Millie's gone. I tried to call her mobile but it's been disconnected. How could they do that to us? I kept waking up in the night in a cold sweat, seeing her face as she was driven away. I love her so much. That's it with me and those two. When I've got my own money I'm going to get Millie back and I'm going to look after her. I swear. We don't need them.

Jerome received two important telephone calls that morning. The first, from Egg, saying The RockAteers had sorted out their differences and were ready to talk about a serious agreement. The second was from Alan Clyro, the C.E.O. of Fictitious Records' parent company – essentially Jerome's boss. Earlier on, Alan had received a call from Hans Molander asking Alan to withdraw the The RockAteers' application to tour with The Desert Kings. When Jerome asked Alan for a reason, his boss had been at a complete loss.

"Hans promised another band the slot six months ago and had to put his foot down with The Desert King's agent. I made it clear you had already offered the slot on the say so of Cab Jones but he told me in no uncertain terms that if we didn't comply, if you tried to contact The Desert Kings direct or kicked up a fuss in any way, it would have serious and far-reaching consequences."

Jerome had met Hans on three or four occasions and this just didn't seem the sort of thing he would do. "Serious and far reaching consequences"? The words, and the demand that The RockAteers should give up on a chance of going on a huge tour, had plagued Jerome all day. It didn't make any sense, Cab Jones would have known if another band had been promised the slot. Besides that, Jerome had never heard of a support slot being offered a year before a tour.

Before Alan had hung up, he stressed that under no circumstances should Jerome ring up his friend Cab or attempt to go over Hans Molander's head. Jerome agreed, but he still needed to find out what the hell had just happened. He had never been gagged by a superior before, even when he had been at the bottom of the ladder. For the first time in his life he felt vulnerable.

For the best part of the day Jerome had sat silently in his chair trying to figure out what was going on, not to speak of how he was going to break the news to The RockAteers. Suddenly from the office radio he heard the distinct singing voice of Lily Vendetta, and a light bulb flashed inside his head. This was the work of Sir Wilson Cloom.

How had Cloom found out? The offer to tour had been a gentlemen's agreement between him and Cab. As far as he knew Wilson and Cab were not friendly. He knew going up against Wilson was professional suicide. He had lost the battle. He needed to concentrate on winning the war.

Winning the war was signing The RockAteers and making them a global success. Stick to what you know, Jerome, he told himself. Tell the truth. Tell The RockAteers that The Desert Kings tour isn't going to happen. Find them another tour, an even better one, before you break the news.

Burt – 10th September
I spent four days at home. Linda tried to make me eat but I wouldn't. Then on the fifth day Mills emailed me. She is up in Scotland. She's not happy, but she's safe. I was so glad I blubbed for a whole half hour. She asked me to promise not to worry, to keep doing the band and that she loves me. I wrote back telling her that she is the best sister in the universe.

For the first time in a week I rang Sophia. I'd been ignoring everyone's calls but I am gonna

do what Millie says and get on with it. Anyway
Sophia came round. She is so fit but I'm getting
a bit bored with her going on about stuff all the
time. It's all a load of bollocks now Mills is
gone. I wish I had Bex. If I had Bex things would
be a bit better. Sophia is really complimentary
about my singing but I'm not an idiot. I know
she's trying to make me sign with Big Tone.
She is going to be given an A&R job there, she
reckons. She told me Jerome Clincher is a liar
and has let loads of bands down. We're going to
see Jerome soon, so I will ask him about it then.

Truth is, I'm getting a bit bored with Sophia,
full stop and think it's about time I make my
move on Bex again. She has hardly spoken to me
since we kissed, and everything has gone all
hectic since then anyway. When we snogged it
was the best five minutes of my life. Until she
suddenly stared at me with this strange look on
her face and stumbled away. I just can't work
her out. One minute she is giving me the signals
and the next she shuts the door in my face. I
looked at a calendar the other day and worked
out I've been in love with her for exactly six
years now. I think if I can't be with her then my
life really won't be worth living. Things are bad
enough as it is.

Crazel is still leaving fifty messages on my phone
a day but at least she doesn't come round the
house any more. The other week she came round and
Sophia answered the door wearing not very much. I
couldn't see them but I could hear them. They had
this sort of bitch-off where Crazel said: "Who
are you?" And Sophia said: "No. Who are you?"
Anyway Sophia told her that she was my girlfriend
and could Crazel please leave me alone because I

think she is a weirdo with saggy boobs (I never said that her boobs were saggy.). Crazel didn't say anything back and Sophia shut the door in her face. I only listened to one of Crazel's messages after that happened, the first one, and to be honest it was really sad. She just told me that she loved me and that she was really upset and why didn't I just tell her that she couldn't see me any more and she thought that we got on really well.

I bloody knew that she'd fallen in love with me! George reckons I should send her a really harsh email telling her to piss off. Cruel to be kind. I'm a bit undecided. One thing's for sure, when Bex finally comes to her senses and realises that we're meant for each other, like Romeo and Juliet, all the other girls in my life are out the window!

Egg – 20th October
Being back at school has been pretty chilled out. I chose A-Level Music, Maths and English, but I'm not doing that much work and don't even have to go in every day. My mum wanted me to do four, but I said no. It's liberating being sixteen.

Band practice has been good. We upped it to five rehearsals a week and it's paying off. We're still allowed to use the school hall and store our stuff in Mr Andrews' music room.

I just had the oddest phone call with Jerome. He

said that he was just making sure that we were
meeting, then he asked me whether Burt is still
in contact with Wilson. I told him I didn't know,
but I wouldn't put anything past him. Then he
asked me who my dream band to go on tour with
was, and I told him The Desert Kings. He said,
No, what would be *MY* favourite band of all time
to go on tour with, so I say "Led Zeppelin". He
went quiet and told me he would see me at the
meeting and hung up.

I'm really excited about going clubbing tonight.
I've never been clubbing before. I nearly told
Bex that I loved her the other day but then I
thought better of it. What if she laughs in my
face? That wouldn't be so good.

Bex and I still haven't told Burt we're together.

Clipper - 26th October
Year Twelve is well easy and we don't need to
wear school uniform. I went out with Bex and
Egg last night. They're proper brilliant those
two. Egg is really egg-ceptional. I chatted to
Bex all about fashion and she was well clued up.
Egg didn't care that I was chatting up his bird
all night. She knew loads of stuff and I learned
loads of stuff. I like dancing, but Bex said I
dance like an old git.

It's a shame Burt couldn't come out. I think
it's about time he knew about Bex and Egg. I feel
a bit sorry for Burt. Since his sister went to

boarding school in Scotland he's all on his own in that massive house. I can't imagine what that must be like.

It was a bit touch and go with my dad for a little while, but I think he's forgiven me for not going to Football Academy. Although he did reapply on my behalf for next season and I got in again! Turns out I do got unbelievable tekkers! I invited Burt round to mine but he told me not to be daft. Anyway UP THE ROCKaTEERS. Me and Egg decided that next year is going to be our year. I cannot wait.

"Sophia said you were a liar! And you are!" Burt declared. "Lads, come on, let's get out of here," he added, eyeballing his band mates.

Jerome and the band were having lunch in The Tabernacle pub on Great Portland Street. The place served great food, and it was Jerome's treat. The meeting, up until that point, had gone well.

"Wait a second, Jack. Who in the hell is Sophia?" Jerome asked.

"She's Sir Wilson Cloom's secretary, if you must know, and she told me that you were a liar, and I didn't believe her, but now I do!"

"OK, wait a moment," said Jerome, raising a calming hand in an effort to stop Burt storming out. "Let me just figure this out for a second. Burt, did you tell Sophia that you were thinking of signing with me? Did you tell her that you were going on tour with The Desert Kings?"

Burt squirmed in his seat uncomfortably. "Not sure… I don't think I remember … I might have… Why? What has that got to do with anything?"

"Well, let me see, Burt. Logic might suggest that if you told her that you were thinking of signing with me, and were going on tour with The Desert Kings, then she might conceivably have told Wilson Cloom the same thing. I think even you can guess the rest?"

"Are you saying," said Egg after a moment's hush, "that Wilson took away our chance to play with The Kings?"

"I'm not suggesting anything of the kind and you would do well never to repeat that insinuation." A smile forming in the foliage of Jerome's generous beard. "You lot really must have pissed Wilson off! I love it. OK, here's what I think we should do…"

Tea – 1st November
Jerome is a good guy! He came up with a wicked plan to stop The Cloominator doing us over. I think because Burt was at the centre of Jerome's plan he calmed down quicker than usual. I swear he's bi-polar or something.

I spose the bottom line is Burt is built to be a front man. Arrogant, egotistical and basically a complete nob. I've read all the rock'n'roll biographies about famous bands and that's exactly what you need from your lead singer. A total nob.

Wilson eyed the pair suspiciously. That he took the meeting in the first place suddenly seemed a huge mistake. He was proud of his re-hiring record. Not one single employee had ever been re-employed. Yet here he was, staring across his desk at Billy Visconti. Wilson's father had been a financier on the stock market and had drummed proverbs, maxims and adages into the young Cloom from an early age. The one that sprang to mind now was: "Never get back into a cold bath". Yet here he was, the cold bath confronting him.

Wilson knew his obsession with signing The RockAteers was clouding his judgement, but he seemed unable to fight the temptation to take the meeting. Besides, he told himself, it had been just this sort of obsession that had propelled him to become the most powerful person in the music industry.

"Sorry," he said, his tone deliberately off-hand. "I don't understand what's happening here."

"OK. Let me put it another way, Sir," said Billy. "The RockAteers think Jerome Clincher is a liar, and have reconsidered their position. If you re-hire me, then the band will sign to Big Tone."

Since his departure from Big Tone Records things had gone from bad to worse for Billy. The same people who would have eaten their own spleen to help Billy only a few months before wouldn't even listen to his messages. Every door he knocked on was closed. Not only had Wilson sacked him, he had managed to blacklist him too.

Wilson turned to Burt. "Is this true, Jack?" he asked.

"We are really sorry and really want to sign with you," Burt replied submissively.

The look of suspicion faded from Wilson's face as the lure of the conquest returned. "Well then!" A smile of triumph. "That *is* good news!" He turned to Billy. "I just can't see what this has to do with you, Billy."

"They won't sign the deal unless I A&R the project," he told his ex-boss a little less confidently.

Wilson lent back in his chair and considered for a moment. "Done," he said, getting to his feet and holding out an open palm. Nodding with obvious relief, Billy grasped it and turned towards Burt.

"Would you mind waiting outside for a moment, Jack? I need to have a quick word with Wilson alone."

Burt nodded, stood up and sloped out of the office.

"I want a raise," Billy told Wilson once he heard the door shut. "I said I would land The RockAteers and I did." There was a silence before Wilson replied.

"OK. A five per cent raise. But Billy... " He paused to maximise the blow. "If this doesn't come off, I am going to *bury you.*"

Billy smiled awkwardly "I have to hand it to you, boss. You really stuck it to that fool Jerome Clincher. Fictitious Records were a shoe-in to sign The RockAteers. How the hell did you do it?"

"It's not *what* you know, Billy," Wilson said with a surreptitious wink.

"But how did you do it, boss? The ink was hovering over the contracts. It was a sure thing!"

Wilson tapped his nose. "A combination of worker bees doing exactly what they are told, and king bees accepting who has the most powerful sting!"

Billy was looking confused. "I don't follow, boss."

"Jesus, Visconti. I've just re-employed you. The least you could do is pretend you're smart enough to keep up with me." Wilson sighed. "OK. I'll give you the simpleton's version… Sophia, my loyal worker bee, gathered all the information I needed from that idiot out there." Cloom pointed through glass at Burt sitting on the couch outside. "Then she planted a seed of doubt in regard to Jerome and his honesty. After that, all I had to do was pull the trigger!"

"Come on, Sir, you can't leave me hanging like that. What did you do?"

Wilson chuckled. "OK, OK. I basically told a less powerful King Bee, Hans Molander, that if he didn't put paid to The RockAteers' tour with The Desert Kings I would make his life a living hell. I knew once Jerome was established as a liar I would be back in the game." Cloom paused. "Of course I didn't expect the game to include you, Visconti, but then I suppose one does need to be flexible on occasion!"

"Well, you certainly are a genius, Sir. I doff my cap." Billy bowed his head in tribute before rising to his feet, experience telling him the meeting was over.

Clipper – 6th November

I met Bex on High Bench yesterday and all of a sudden I just started talking about stuff. I told her about George calling me a batty man in front of everyone and she got proper angry and told me that she thought George Graves was a nasty

bastard. She asked me if I was gay. I just told
her that I thought I was. I couldn't look at her
when I told her, because to be honest, actually
saying it out loud was still just about the
hardest thing I've ever done. I don't know what I
expected. Maybe I thought she would laugh in my
face, but of course she didn't. She was proper
lovely and caring, I just went all the way and
then told her that I sorta had feelings for Burt
for ages but now I didn't have feelings for him
any more, mainly coz he's a total dick head. I
felt really good letting it all out. She told me
that I was the loveliest and kindest person she
had ever met.

That's when I cried, and in between weeping I told
her how scared I was about telling my mum and dad.
My dad especially, telling my old man his eldest
son is gay might push him over the edge. Whilst I
was sniffling Bex told me I should be more worried
about telling my dad I used to fancy the centre
forward of my school football team!

I love Bex. I wish I fancied her because I would
proper steal her away from Egg.

Tea − 9th November
I gotta put this down. It was absolute quality.
Me and George and about ten others were up the
park after school just chillin. As usual George
was tellin us jokes about some of the kids in
school. We were all sittin about chillin' but
George was stood up facing us.

When I spot Bex walking up behind him she puts
her fingers to her lips and we all keep schtum.
George wears his jeans pretty baggy. So anyway,
she walks up behind him and pulls down his
trousers and pants in one move.

George just stands there with his nob and balls
swinging in the air. It took exactly one second
before we all started pissing ourselves. Turns
out that George hasn't got the massive wanger
he's banged on about.

George falls over trying to pull his jeans back up
and we all crease up even more. It was brilliant
because at that very moment Clipper showed up.
After all the grief he's taken he deserved to see
George being humiliated. It's only a shame Egg
wasn't there too. Then Bex's words come floating
over as she starts walking off.

"You're an 'orrible little bully, George Graves,
and now everyone knows the dick on your head is
way bigger than the one in your pants."

A vicious look came over George's face and before
any of us can stop him he runs up behind her and
punches her in the back of the head. Bex flew
forward and landed on the grass in a heap. None
of us could believe it.

I wasn't having it. My dad hit my mum when I was
little and I will never forget it. So I stood up
and ran at him. Just as I was about to get my
shot away George goes down in a heap right in
front of me – from a massive right hook delivered
by Clipper. What a total legend you are, Clip!
The man is pure gold.

Next day in school Bex comes up and gives us both
a peck on the cheek and says she heard Clip only
just beat me to it. We're her knights in shining
armour. She also let me feel the big bump on the
back of her head (and that was even better than
the kiss, which I know is weird).

I tell you what. If Egg wasn't going out with her
I would be getting on one knee and proposing.

"Is that Sophia?" Jerome asked, trying to keep his voice steady.

"Who is this, please?" Sophia received around twenty calls a day from unsigned acts looking to talk to Wilson.

"It's Jerome Clincher. We've never met but you might know of me. I'm the guy you set up."

"Oh… God … look … I never meant to… "

"Save it. Put your boss on the line."

"Er … I'm not sure he will take the call… "

"If you don't put him on the phone right now, Sophia, I will come down to the office and publicly humiliate you."

The phone went dead. Jerome wondered if she had hung up.

"Cloom here."

"Jerome Clincher."

"Oh. Have you rung to concede defeat?"

"Actually, I called to say that I have just heard a very interesting recording." Jerome savoured the moment. "It's audio of a meeting you had with Billy Visconti and Jack Skill a few days ago."

Jerome waited for a reaction, none came and he continued. "The recording seems to suggest that you might have had something to do with ruining a support tour I set up for The RockAteers."

The line went silent. "And?" Cloom said eventually.

"And … if you don't get me back that support tour and leave The RockAteers and my company alone, then I'm going to send the tape to my pal Jordan at The Daily Blog."

"I must warn you, Jerome," said Wilson, after a pause. "Going up against me will have serious consequences. The main consequence being that I will bury you alive."

"I hoped you might say something like that." Jerome replied. "You'll be comforted to hear I'm recording this call also… Thank you for being so utterly predictable, Sir Wilson."

"Send your silly little tape recordings to the press, I don't care. I think you've failed to grasp the kind of power I wield. I am untouchable."

"Think for a moment, Sir Wilson. You might still be rich and powerful, sure, but how would you front your precious family TV shows, if this stuff got leaked? Being 'Wicked Wilson' the pantomime villain is one thing. Being a ruthless deceitful tycoon is another thing entirely." He paused. "Have you got the message? *Leave me and my band alone."*

Silence.

"What do you want?" Wilson grunted. "Money?"

"Repeat after me: 'I promise to leave you and your band alone'."

After a further silence, Jerome said: "I'm putting the phone down in three seconds. One, two…"

"Yes, OK. OK. I will leave you and your band alone!"

"Thank you. Oh, and one last thing. If you sack Billy Visconti again, the same thing happens. I send the tape. Got it?"

Jerome hung up before Cloom could answer. He picked the receiver up again and dialled Egg's number.

Burt – 17th November

Jerome is such a total ledge. Me and the boys went to see him yesterday and he told us the tour with The Desert Kings is back on. I absolutely can't wait to blow those biatches off stage. He also offered us the record deal and all of us were well excited (about bloody time). Jerome said if it wasn't for me we wouldn't have been able to escape the Cloominater. All the boys gave me a big cheer (also about bloody time).

The signing party is in a month's time, with a gig on the same night. It's on a really posh boat that I've seen going down the river a million times. Millie is coming. She checked with Mum and she can come down because her Christmas holidays will have started. I cannot wait to see her. I've decided I'm going to tell Bex that I love her on that night. I worked it all out the day after I split up from Sophia. #checklisttime

1. I think about her all the time.
2. I think about the snog we had all the time.
3. She is really really fit.
4. I love her.

Jerome had attended four rehearsals since The RockAteers had agreed to sign with his label. Each time his faith and enthusiasm in the band was renewed and reinforced. The new crop of songs he'd heard were incredible. The band trusted him now; he had proved himself. Jerome had recognised early on that this bunch needed to see his commitment with their own eyes. Of course he wouldn't have guessed in a million years how the finale would play out. He had never worked harder to secure a band in his life.

It was the night of the signing party. Jerome had invited rock stars from some of the biggest bands in the UK, a selection of top-notch journalists, as well as key figures from the entertainment world. Everyone wanted to see what the talented Mr Clincher would come up with next. Jerome felt sure The RockAteers would be his crowning glory.

The Silver Sturgeon looked amazing; the plush, modern interior was grand without being pretentious. Moored at Savoy pier on the Embankment, its location was ideal for London's rock'n'roll elite. As Jerome passed through the empty boat he felt confident. The sound-check had gone really well, and the setting was cool and unusual. Not many bands performed gigs whilst floating down the Thames, through the heart of one of the coolest cities in the world.

He gazed out of a porthole. The guests were starting to arrive, tottering up the gang-plank in their glad-rags. Jerome headed upstairs to the large open-air deck, the brackish river air greeting him as he arrived on the promenade. He lingered by the entrance for a moment, watching the band as they laughed and joked with one another. What a crazy, talented and innocent bunch they were. What must it be like to be sixteen and about to have a huge party in your honour?

"All set?" Jerome said, greeting them with a warm smile.

"Locked and loaded, Roma!" Tea replied with a grin.

"Roma?" Jerome asked puzzled.

"Jerome … Rome … Roma. It's your new nickname."

"Roma, eh?" he smiled. "I can think of worse nicknames. Anyway, you're on in an hour, OK?" He tapped his watch and made his way back below deck to greet the guests.

Bex arrived just as Jerome left, her outfit rendering the band speechless. When she saw Egg, she beamed, ran over and flung her arms around him, kissing him full on the mouth.

"What's going on?" Burt asked, taking a step toward the entwined couple, his face twisted in confusion.

Egg tried in vain to untangle himself from Bex. "Er…" Egg looked at Clipper for support, but everyone was staring at Burt.

"You OK about this?" Bex said, turning toward Burt, remaining cheek to cheek with Egg. "I told him you wouldn't have a problem with it."

"Problem? Why would I have a problem?" Burt choked.

"That's a relief then." Bex held Egg close.

Burt stared out over the choppy water of the river Thames. "I'm going to the dressing room to warm my voice up now," he said mechanically. "My vocal coach told me that it was really important to warm up."

Burt shook his head to displace the building sweat and peered into the gloom. The only thing he could see was the outline of heads as the stage lights blinded his view. He had no idea what they were screaming and he didn't care. Mills hadn't turned up. It was the most miserable day of his life. Turning, he glimpsed his drummer's face, gaping with exhaustion. Clipper winked, clicked his sticks four times, shoed his bass drum pedal and the band plunged into their final song, "Golden".

The show finished to a hail of whistles and screams. Burt hurled his microphone stand into the crowd and strode off stage. As he walked briskly to the exit he heard the crowd roaring for an encore. He reached outside, the salty air fresh against his sweat-drenched face and discovered the boat was back at the pier. As he staggered up the gang-plank, his stomach lurched. He bent over, placed his hands on his haunches and heaved his guts up into the Thames.

"Had a bit too much to drink?" enquired a mocking voice. Burt peered behind him, frowned and waved the man away. "I just have a couple of questions."

"Piss off, I'm busy."

"What do you think about when you are on stage, Jack Skill?"

"Who are you?"

"I'm with The Daily Blog. Jerome invited me."

Burt straightened up, wiped his mouth and tried to make the man out in the gloom.

"What do I think about? I think about all the girls looking at me, how's that?"

Before the journalist could respond, Burt heard a more familiar voice.

"Are you all right?"

"Crazel!" Burt gasped.

"The gig was amazing, I just can't believe how far you've come. The new songs are fantastic." She started to rub his back.

"I don't want to be … look, can't you leave me alone?"

Undeterred, Hazel held on to him, leaning her head close to his. "There's something you need to know Burt. I'm pregnant. I'm not lying and I'm going to have the baby!" she whispered. "You can ignore me all you like, but I'm in your life now, forever. Get used to it. I'm not going anywhere."

The wave of horror that swept over Burt was like nothing he had ever experienced before. With a sudden jerk of his body, he shrugged her off and zig-zagged up the gang-plank. "You can run but you can't hide from this!" Hazel called after him. "You have no idea who my dad is do you? Watch your back!" was the last thing he heard as he reached the street and fled into the night.

Burt arrived back at the house just after midnight. He paid the cab driver and trudged up the marble stairs. He took a quick shower, pulled on a fresh pair of skinny jeans and padded down to the kitchen shirtless. He liberated a beer from the refrigerator, hesitated and replaced it, before going directly to his father's study and opening the drinks cabinet. He chose a bottle of vodka, sat down at his father's solid oak bureau desk, took a giant swig and began to sob.

For two hours he wept, between long draughts of booze,

before standing up, placing the vodka under his arm, and staggering back to the kitchen. He wished Millie was there, but she wasn't. His mum must have gone back on her word, probably just to spite them both.

"Bitch," he muttered as he lurched through the kitchen.

Burt headed straight for the medicine cabinet, rifled through its contents until he found a bottle of his mother's antidepressant pills. He unscrewed the cap and poured the contents down his throat, washing it down with a large slug of vodka. He leant against the fridge and slid on to the kitchen floor.

His mobile phone went off again, another text alert. He had ignored all the texts and calls he had received that night but this one he decided to open. It was from Clipper.

HEAD OF SONY USA WAS @GIG. HE LOVED IT AND
THINKS WE ARE GOING TO BE HUGE IN THE US. HOPE
YOUR OK MATE.U LEFT REAL QUICK? BTW YOUR LITTLE
MILLIE JUST TURNED UP! COME BACK!

Burt sprung to his feet as if struck by lightning. He dropped the bottle and shoved his fingers down his throat. Nothing. In a blind panic he sprinted back to the study, grabbed the car keys from the bowl on his Dad's desk and staggered towards the front door.

The car lurched out of the drive as he over-steered and bumped up the opposite curb. He managed to return to the road and set off toward the hospital. He made it as far as Blackheath Hill before blacking out, scraping along four cars and ploughing into a garden wall.

The ambulance arrived ten minutes later.

BONUS TRACK WAKING THE DEAD

Clipper – 20th December
We got the news about Burt the next morning. The
only thing he had in his pockets that identified
him was an old gig flier. Amazingly, a nurse
looked the band up on the hospital computer and
sent us an email. Egg picked it up and rang us
all. I think he felt really bad about the whole
thing. I do reckon him and Bex could have found a
better way to tell Burt they were together.

Millie was just dumped at the gig by some fella
in a Range Rover, and then with Burt gone she had
no one to look after her, so Bex took her back to
her house. She covered up the whole Burt drama
until Egg called us really early the next day.

We took Millie down the hospital and waited for
him to wake up. We didn't have to wait that long.
He's a tough kid our Burt. As soon as he saw
Millie he started smiling and then right after
that he started bawling. I've never seen two
people hug each other so tight. They were crying
so much they had me joining in! What would we do
for drama if we didn't have Burt? I'm just so
glad he didn't die. No one else was there for
him. As far as I know he didn't even get a phone
call from either his mum or dad. How can people
be like that?

I don't know if I'm talking rubbish or not but I think Burt trying to do himself in put everything into perspective. I started feeling better about myself, less guilty, more positive. So what if I'm gonna be a gay rock star instead of a gay footballer. I'm loving life and I think that's what it's all about really!

Tea – 24th February
You couldn't make it up! Captain Burk and the rock'n'roll death wish. One day when I'm old I will look back on these days and wish I could have them all back again. Only I would have them slower and in 3D. Since Burt got out of hospital we've been working on the band nonstop. Clipper reckons Burt's overdose might have been the best thing that ever happened to the band – like it galvanized us or something. Either way, The RockAteers has never been more enjoyable. We all got a couple of grand to tide us over until our record advance comes in. I will pay Uncle Frank back. He will try to turn it down but I will insist. It will be the first honest money he has ever handled. LOL.

Egg – 15th March
"Suicide is a permanent solution to a temporary problem." Phil Donahue (Talk show host)

I have come to realise that Burt is the strangest
man ever to grace this earth. He will not under
any circumstances acknowledge Bex and I are
having a relationship. At first it was difficult,
because I would mention her in rehearsals or in
the studio, but then once I cottoned on that
it was completely off limits, I just stopped
mentioning her altogether, a temporary solution
to a permanent problem.

Even before Burt tried to kill himself there
was loads of hype. Now it's absolutely mental.
I think his mum being Claudia Windsor the
supermodel contributed. I had no idea she was
famous. He never ever talks about his parents. I
thought our Twitter and Facebook couldn't swell
any bigger. Now we have more online followers,
fans and friends than Holland has citizens. When
Jerome said it like that it really hit home.
Burt's suicide-attempt was the greatest PR stunt
we could have pulled, except it was real.

I had to give up my A-Levels when we signed the
deal. My mum went absolutely ballistic. I was
so upset, Bex suggested I could use the money
Jerome gave us to move out. So that's what
I'll do. I'm going to rent a nice little flat in
Blackheath. It's going to be so liberating. Mum
was absolutely flabbergasted when I told her. It
wasn't easy. Jerome will have to sign my tenancy
agreement. Mum threatened me with court action
because officially I need permission to move out,
but Dad had a word with her and she dropped
it. Good old Dad. If anything me and Mum's
relationship has got better since.

In the end I decided I would split the publishing
equally. It was Bex who changed my mind. She

said if the lads coming on the adventure with me are resentful then what's the point? I told The RockAteers yesterday. They cheered, grabbed me and gave me the bumps. Even Burt!

When I think back 18 months and try and grasp how much my life has changed I struggle. From a miserable geek on the wrong side of the canteen to this! I'm not watching the world pass me by any more. I'm a proper part of it. How did that happen?! Bex reckons it's because I believed in myself and worked hard at the thing I love, music. Maybe she's right. Either way, I got the girl and I love what I do. I'm the luckiest man alive.

Jack Skill – 30th March
I am fully pumped. In a few weeks everyone on the planet will know my name and #rockateers will be doing some proper mental trending! What do you think about that, Dad? You nasty bastard. You can stick your "style over substance" up your arse. The music sounds awesome. Live show is slick as shizzle and I've finally worked it out. Bex didn't want any old deadbeat in a band, she wanted a bona fide rock star. Exactly what I'm gonna be before the year is out. Never say die.

I've got the plan for me and Millie all sorted too. It's all gonna work out. Although from her emails I get the feeling she quite likes that school she's at. She is still pretty annoyed at me for trying to do myself in. Thank God I didn't die. What a loss for humanity it would have been.

Crazel is gonna have the baby and it's a boy!
She's seven months gone. I didn't bother having a
sperm test. I'm pretty sure it's mine. Now I've
got my head round it, it's actually pretty wicked!

Never in a million years could I have guessed
all the shit that has gone down since I started
The RockAteers. But one thing is for sure. I was
proper certain that any band I invented was gonna
be absolutely massive. Talent guided by genius
can achieve anything.

ACKNOWLEDGEMENTS

Big the love to M&D for being awesome partners. To Penny for pushing me further. To Jimbo and all his dope skill. To Lil Al and Ben for keeping the faith. To Rodz for all that belief. And finally my family who are everything.

THE ROCK'N'ROLL DIARIES

I want to thank all the amazing people who have read, listened, supported, edited, knitted dolls, decorated shoes, sent me letters, collages, mailed me gifts and showed so much love that a man might feel utterly overwhelmed.

Below is a list of Twitter handles that you should go follow coz they are awesome. They are the people who have made this whole crazy vibe a reality. There ARE many more of you that have been wicked so if you're not on the list then sorry. There is always book 2...

So, massive thanks to...

@ItsSam91
@SuzannePushTen
@proudscriptette
@unforgiven1964
@Saaaartjjj
@gisellenolan
@SarahBlackie1
@shannonnewman92
@Natwritesstuff
@JaydeScriptette
@MollyWoodward_
@emmalhanks
@5secsofnarryx_

@IfYouSeeGabbie
@ScriptLoveUK
@MrLuqman_
@Xerxes_027
@BoroLou
@LauraLClayton
@sarah_fowler_x
@LM_ScriptBeat
@MelindaTSQ
@Lauren2926
@dewilvb
@borolou
@lupuspitasari

@violemunram
@rianne_smelt
@GlenPowerfanpag
@paula_script
@AndaAndrijanic
@Mummystars
@OlixWilliams
@TL_dc
@TheScript_Kiana
@Bamms
@IfYouSeeFebri
@Huggy77
@andy_TK8

@TheScriptSK
@scriptette007
@dionnejayne91
@ScriptObsessive
@mirelagric
@TheScriptlovex
@AnjoliColar
@giselleolan
@LynseyAllington
@claudia_barner
@alberta87
@koalabeaxo
@DairyOfATeacher
@gjeel
@jennahrator
@deepadley78
@Kayy_85
@C0YWM
@FABRIZIA226
@n0goodingoodbye
@NicolaRoberts87
@tlc4mb20SCRIP
@CharleyDolan1
@millie_lol
@isa_abrantes
@ThescriptXfan
@adeleroberts79
@Claire_M_Fowler
@Andrea1025
@reneeadd75
@vkrivogornitsy3
@craignichola
@juleerandy
@bethanywXx
@sxphiemeyer
@hannahayden3
@xlizzymac
@IfYouSee_Rachel
@tsaremyangels

@ImWithTheScript
@daria91rocks
@scriptette1400
@mymoonwish
@NicolaReddican
@MusicfanAndrea
@thescriptlyric4
@zaraxcb
@TheMouse214
@TheScriptEdit
@ThescriptB
@TheScriptAmy
@sharonpower66
@StefaniaByanka
@alexistaft
@foxyshell007
@lxstgalaxy
@misskeeleywhite
@badluck_glen
@bef0rethew0rst_
@_xCatherinex_
@courtneyyxoall
@FerrisMillie
@Moonboots1712
@kayla__sale
@maddie_mcfc
@BekahLou_Martin
@Me_L_Bo
@iCutileiro
@fxckwillis
@thescript_zoe
@carlylouisetur1
@LawsonArgOfi
@CarolinenaaL
@donny_kebab
@ArielleTubbs
@lifesjustablink
@danni0782
@_T4NN3R

@Alonso_Mateo_
@NesbianOfNY
@enaaaax
@DiannaDia24
@bellebobean
@wee_emss
@KellHolmes
@Beforetheworst3
@Nre18
@OneMaroonScript
@ChloeScriptette
@ThisIsLove81
@emilyanna_q
@RobCav08
@_fragilerose
@upside_ahead
@ginoplus3
@mollydobson2
@pushLeigh
@melissamellett
@lucypresley123
@karenadavey72
@CloserCloser_
@FernValentine
@tanyathomas82
@Amanda_Mck_
@nidges_missus
@gigtripper86
@nowords99
@SarahHallahan1
@tigs5
@mornrose
@LottieLewis_
@omglukeslipring
@SiljeOostwounder
@tinswizzle
@jennajones86
@Thescript_Nat
@24_7baby365

@Limana68
@careymoore18
@ScriptGirlPDX
@MackemClaire
@blondieboo77
@senyorandannie
@HelR10
@anjuli_x
@yunchien
@SineadOnAWire
@ScriptSyndrome
@Missandi0623
@alicefennxll
@xJulieLeeSx_MG
@Kezzii1
@lindadannys
@bellaolipia
@mandyscfc
@_LadyNadia
@Tezzozzz
@recesinque
@Mumikoj
@Gigs_and_nails
@lynjhen
@lottie2511
@Nutterpw
@x_hannah_x_x

@ItsZacharyT
@__EHFAR__
@lolly3085
@Terrie86
@marsyita46
@Lunda_ox
@_natwhitehouse
@CJT_78
@Mrs_ODonoghue
@Dannys_Tiger
@JuztYvonne
@AJLthescript
@Leonadorney_TS
@_daniallan
@Jellie_baby
@AnnieHH1987
@lifesawitch
@Georgina_Dolan
@catbyme_
@Musicangel1712
@TheScriptCrazy
@revampedrebel
@wirechick
@StephGuiness
@Paddy5
@sarah4s
@TSQuotesMR

@JoB1607
@Lottiie
@IvannaC
@cindytb_
@didicon74
@If_youcouldsee
@megggge
@annii_thescript
@LaurenNSWS
@Han_brookhallRD
@meganerlam
@kodaroxox
@GlenSuperPower
@The_ScriptNinja
@Roxanaxox
@oneyoungvolcano
@AndreaCheyenne7
@Nads_Pichler
@anto_scripter
@Jess_thescript
@AnaMaria3133
@d0ntwaitforluck
@beccagriff22
@Joana_Stefo
@ArnoldJHaidu
@may_midge

About
the Author

Jamie Scallion grew up in South East London. He spent twelve years writing, recording and touring in a band. Whilst on the road he wrote The Rock 'n' Roll Diaries.

Photo © Ami Barwell

THE ROCK'N'ROLL DIARIES

LOOK OUT FOR BOOK TWO:

HAVING IT

COMING SOON

16496799R00139

Printed in Great Britain
by Amazon